WHISPERS
in the Wind

The Shadow Creek Ranch Series

WHISPERS
in the Wind

Charles Mills

REVIEW AND HERALD® PUBLISHING ASSOCIATION
HAGERSTOWN, MD 21740

This book was
Edited by Raymond H. Woolsey
Designed by Bill Kirstein
Cover illustration by Joe Van Severen
Type set: 12/14 Century Book

PRINTED IN U.S.A.

98 97 96 95 94 93   10 9 8 7 6 5 4 3 2 1

R&H Cataloging Service
Mills, Charles Henning, 1950-
    Whispers in the wind.

    I. Title.

        813.54

ISBN 0-8280-0811-6

Dedication

To the Harold Kuebler clan—
In-laws *extraordinaire*!

Contents

imaginations? It's nothing as exciting as all that. But it is a mystery. Come, I'll show you."

The woman led the ever-curious youngsters into the bedroom and paused before the closet door. "There," she said, pointing into the dark shadows of the small enclosure. "Would you mind telling me what that is, and how it got in here?"

Joey drew in his breath as his mouth dropped open. "My geologist's pick. MY GEOLOGIST'S PICK! I've been looking everywhere for it. How did—" He stopped in mid-sentence. The boy's eyes narrowed as he slowly turned to face one of his companions. "Wendy Hanson?" he said in as pleasant a tone as possible, considering his teeth were clenched together tightly. "As I recall, and correct me if I'm wrong, I seem to remember loaning you that very geo-pick about two months ago. And," he lifted his work-soiled index finger as if to make a point, "you *promised* to bring it back."

The lad's voice began to tremble. "Wrangler Barry thinks that I lost it. Me. He says I left it somewhere. ME! Now, here's my geo-pick on the closet floor of Mrs. Dawson's house up here in the middle of the Gallatin National Forest. I know I ain't the smartest person in the world, and I may be from New York City, but would I be too far out of line to ask you for an explanation?"

Wendy smiled meekly. "Joey, Joey, Joey. You can ask me anything you'd like. We're friends. Buddies. Like brother and sister."

"The only thing we are right now is mortal enemies," the boy said, taking a step toward Wendy. The girl didn't budge.

"Just calm down, Mr. Dugan," she said. "I can explain everything."

"I'm listening," came the icy reply.

"Well." Wendy blinked her eyes, trying to look innocent and sweet. "You see, when I found that board out on the road that had 'Merrilee' written on it and when I couldn't get through the wall of underbrush and vines, I got mad and threw the geo-pick at it."

"You threw my geologist's pick at a bunch of vines and underbrush?"

"And trees," Wendy added. "There were lots of trees, too."

Joey closed his eyes.

"But I missed," the girl brightened even further. "That silly ol' geo-pick sailed right over that silly ol' barrier and that's when I heard it."

"Heard what?" Joey asked, his voice not much above a whisper.

"The glass breaking. SMASH—tinkle, tinkle. That's when I knew I'd really found something neat."

Mr. Dawson turned and studied the window pane he'd just replaced. He then looked across the room at the closet. Yup. The two were right in line with the tangle of vines near the road.

"So," the girl concluded, "I guess that geo-pick came right in through the window and landed in the closet and . . . so . . . there it is." She reached down and picked up the tool. "Here's your geologist's pick, Mr. Dugan," she said, smiling sweetly. "Sorry it took so long to get it back to you. But a promise is a promise."

With that she turned and stepped lightly out into the hallway and descended the stairs.

Merrilee's hand shot to her mouth in an attempt to stifle a laugh. Her husband turned quickly toward the window so Joey wouldn't see his uncontrolled grin.

The boy sighed. "That Wendy is crazy. Totally, off-the-wall crazy." He shook his head and left the room.

Behind him, gales of laughter suddenly exploded, the happy sound echoing through the little rooms and broad-beam rafters of the old homestead. Joey glanced down at Mr. Underfoot. Even the raccoon seemed to be overflowing with giggles as he scurried past the boy and followed Wendy down the stairs.

The youngster sighed again. How was he going to tell Wrangler Barry that he'd found the long-lost geologist's pick in a musty, dark closet on the second floor of an abandoned farmhouse? He brightened. Not to worry. He'd just mention to his ranch-hand boss that he'd loaned the tool to Wendy. That should be explanation enough.

* * * * *

Mr. Hanson steered his red minivan along the

bumpy, mountain road that led from the Station to the old homestead nestled in a fold of the Absaroka Range in southwestern Montana. He hummed an unending tune as he sat watching the last remnants of autumn drop lazily from the passing cottonwoods and aspens.

Even the small stands of white birch moving slowly by the vehicle no longer wore their fall finery. Winter was coming. You could feel it in the October air. You could see it in the frenzied activity of the small forest creatures that lived among the fallen logs and grassy patches of the mountains and meadows.

The lawyer settled back in his seat and let his mind wander freely. So much had happened during the past five months. Shadow Creek Ranch had welcomed its first small group of teenagers from across the country. Joey had surprised everyone and gone back to New York to help his streetwise brother. Wendy had found a farm and a person, both named Merrilee. The Dawsons—Merrilee and her husband—had moved from Stevensville to the farm and were preparing to start their new lives in the old home that the woman's grandmother had willed to them. Debbie had found a part-time job in Bozeman with a company that designed window dressings for department stores. And somehow, through it all, he'd managed to maintain a busy workload at his home office in the old way station.

Life was full. Sometimes too full. But he and his

mom and dad seemed to be holding down the fort with some degree of success. Hadn't Lizzy Pierce said just the other day that life on Shadow Creek Ranch was as overflowing as a mountain stream in spring?

Mr. Hanson nodded. Life was good, and worthwhile. But he secretly hoped that the coming winter would be a time for relaxing, for recharging his inner soul. As during the winter before, the only challenge he wanted to face was making sure the children studied their school lessons and did all that Mrs. Pierce, their housemate-turned-teacher, told them to do.

The little minivan continued up the old logging road, making its way through the tall stands of spruce and fir. Yes, this winter would hold no surprises. As the local grizzlies demonstrated, it was time to hibernate in the warm and cozy den of the Station.

Beep. Beep. Wendy looked up to see her father's vehicle slip through the narrow opening among the trees and come to a stop by the newly painted shed.

She waved and turned back to her work. A new section of porch had recently replaced the old, broken portion by the front door. Her job on this cool Sunday afternoon was to apply a thick coat of white paint over the carefully nailed boards, sealing the wood from the weather.

"You 'bout done?" her father asked as he walked toward the girl. "Looks pretty good around here. I see you've finished the shed. We'll start stacking fire-wood in there tomorrow after school."

"Yup," Wendy smiled with satisfaction as she wiped stray strands of blond hair from her forehead. "Merrilee is lookin' great, just like I knew it would. It's hard work, though. Even Joey looks a little pooped around the eyes."

"I heard that," the boy's voice called from inside the rustic living room. "Ask your daughter what we found upstairs, Mr. H."

The lawyer glanced down at his youngest child. "A pot of gold? A treasure map?"

Wendy rolled her eyes. "No. Joey found his geologist's pick."

"Ask her where it was," invited the bodyless voice from inside.

"Where'd you find it?" Mr. Hanson smiled.

"In the upstairs closet."

"Ask her how it got there."

The lawyer's eyebrows rose. "How'd it get there?"

"Through the window, of course," the girl said, dipping her paintbrush in the container of thick, white liquid beside her knee.

"Ask her who threw it through the window."

"Who th—"

"I did," Wendy interrupted. "So, big deal." She faced the front door. "You've got your stupid ol' pick back, so just forget it."

Mr. Hanson lowered his voice and bent close to his daughter's ear. "So . . . why'd you throw Joey's geologist's pick through the window?"

"I'll tell you later," the girl sighed. "Much later."

The man chuckled. "OK. But now you'd better finish up what you're doing. It'll be dark soon. Supper's waiting down at the Station. Grandma and Lizzy have prepared lentil soup with homemade bread and peach jam."

Wendy unconsciously licked her lips. If there was one thing the girl liked more than a good mystery, it was good food, and lots of it. For someone who'd been eating for only 10 years, she could pack it away with the best of them.

Before long, all the workers had been rounded up, tools washed and put away, and door and windows closed against the night air. As the little red minivan descended the mountain road, it overflowed with tired but happy passengers. The old homestead was almost ready. Before the heavy winter snows arrived, John and Merrilee Dawson would be living within its cozy walls, warmed by the newly-installed wood-burning stove and the memory of the generous old woman who'd lived there many years before.

But for now, only one thought held center stage in the minds of the weary travelers: lentil soup and homemade bread with peach jam. What a delicious way to end the day.

Supper was everything it was hoped to be. Bowls of steaming soup disappeared down hungry throats as pleasant chatter drifted with the sweet smell of freshly baked squash bread.

Samantha sat beside Joey, her dark face radiant with pleasure as she heaped top-heavy piles of jam on her third slice.

"Take it easy, Sam," the boy chuckled. "If you eat anymore you'll pop like a balloon."

The 5-year-old stopped chewing and looked up at her companion. "I will?" she said, her mouth full of bread and jam.

"Yeah. We'll have to scrape you off the walls with a shovel."

"Gross!" Wendy moaned.

Debbie wrinkled her nose. "Come on, Joey. We're trying to eat."

Grandpa Hanson nodded. "We'd have Samantha soup."

"Puh-leeze," Lizzy groaned. "I think I'm getting ill."

Wendy shook her head. "No, no. If she popped we'd have Samantha stew."

Debbie lifted her hand. "Enough already. I happen to like the smallest member of our ranch family all in one piece, if it's OK with the rest of you."

Samantha's little black face grinned a wide, peach-jam grin. "Thank you, Debbie. But I'd make a delicious stew, I think. Dizzy says I'm as sweet as sugar and as yummy as candy cane."

Those gathered around the table burst out laughing at Samantha's evaluation of herself. "You're right," Joey said, smiling. He bent down and gave his adopted sister a wet, slobbery kiss on the cheek, then he licked his lips. "One thing's for sure. You do taste like peaches, for some strange reason."

"See?" the little girl beamed. "Sweet. Just like Dizzy says."

Wrangler Barry entered the room and hurried over to his place at the table. "Sorry I'm late, folks," he apologized as he hurriedly began loading his plate with food. "Had a little trouble with one of the horses." He glanced over at Joey and grinned. "The big black one. Didn't want to come in for the night. Had to chase that beast clean around the pasture."

"Hey," Joey said, lifting his hands palms up. "Tar Boy likes the great outdoors. He doesn't want to be cooped up in some corral with a bunch of sissy horses like . . . oh . . . Early, shall we say."

"Early's not a sissy," Wendy shot back. "He's as tough as that Mack truck you call a horse."

Mr. Hanson cleared his throat. "Wendy? Joey? Let's just eat our food in peace. You two can discuss the merits of your horses later, OK?"

Debbie nodded and smiled shyly over at Wrangler Barry. "That's right, *children*," she said, emphasizing the last word. "Supper is no time for silly, *childish* conversations." She lifted her fork and poised it above the plate. "Barry and I would like to eat our meal in peace and quiet."

The wrangler blinked and looked around the table. "Why, thank you, Miss Debbie," he grinned. "I was just telling the horses how totally disgusting *their* eating habits were. You and I are truly kindred spirits." With that he gingerly lifted his milk glass and took a tiny sip. "Now, please pass the soup, if you would be so kind."

Debbie smiled sweetly. "Certainly." She lifted the large bowl of steaming liquid and was in the process of presenting it to the young ranch hand when her fingers slipped and the container dropped with a plate-shattering thud on the table.

A wave of lentil soup rose from the bowl and washed across Wrangler Barry's face, leaving it coated with the meal's main course.

Debbie's eyes opened wide with horror. The horseman remained seated, seemingly unaffected by the hot bath he'd just received.

"And may I have some bread?" he said with a smile. "It's just not proper to eat soup without a few morsels of bread."

Joey sank into his chair, gales of laughter racking his young, muscular body. Wendy buried her face in her hands and shook uncontrollably. Grandpa and Grandma Hanson and the Dawsons didn't even try to hide their merriment as they joined Mr. Hanson and Dizzy in a roaring response to the ranch hand's composure.

But it was Samantha that finally brought the house down and ended all attempts at sanity. "Hey, look," she called out excitedly. "Now Wrangler Barry's as delicious as I am."

Debbie sat silent and red-faced for the remainder of the meal. As much as she loved Shadow Creek

Ranch and all its inhabitants, human and otherwise, she did wish for a more formal atmosphere from time to time.

But it was the ranch's young wrangler who really got her 17-year-old heart racing. He was tall, slender, with sun-streaked brown hair and the bluest eyes she'd ever seen. Someday, Barry would graduate from Montana State University in Bozeman with a degree in agriculture. He wanted to be a rancher. Debbie fantasized that, maybe, he'd include her in his plans. But so far, she'd only managed to throw him into Shadow Creek and drench him with lentil soup.

During their trips into town, he'd shared his hopes and dreams with the young girl as she sat beside him in his speedy four-wheel-drive pickup truck.

She'd listen intently and nod her head thoughtfully. He even said he enjoyed talking with her. But Debbie was beginning to feel that she'd have a better chance of attracting his attention if she knitted her next sweater out of burlap. Maybe if she'd dab a little "Essence of Horse" behind her ears she might succeed in catching his eye.

"Did I mention that you look lovely this evening?" the wrangler was saying as Debbie blinked back her rambling thoughts. The meal was finished and everyone had left the table. She could hear Lizzy and Wendy busy with the dishes at the kitchen sink. "That's a lovely sweater. Did you make it yourself?"

The girl smiled shyly. "Yes." She ran her hand

along her shoulder and let it follow the curve of her arm down to the sleeve. "I tried to capture the beauty of nature with these little leaves and flowers. Do you really like it?"

Wrangler Barry nodded enthusiastically. "I do, Debbie. You're very talented. I've always admired you . . . uh . . . your work."

"Thanks," she said brightly. "Oh . . . and . . . sorry 'bout the soup."

The ranch hand grinned. "Don't worry your pretty little head about it. No damage done."

He gave her a quick wink and rose to leave. "Gotta get to the university. Grandpa asked me to pick you up Tuesday at the mall and bring you back with me to the ranch. Five o'clock all right?"

"Great," Debbie nodded. "I'll make sure I'm done by then. We're working on that new store, you know, the one beside the Furniture Palace? I'll be waiting for you there."

The horseman grinned and waved. "See ya."

He disappeared through the doorway, leaving Debbie alone. She sat for a long moment in the silence. "See ya," she said softly.

* * * * *

In the weeks that followed, Shadow Creek Ranch fell into its usual routine of work, play, and study. Wendy, Joey, and Debbie labored at their school books as Lizzy Pierce skillfully taught morning classes in the den's cozy home school.

Mr. Hanson busied himself at his computer and fax machine, maintaining a constant stream of information and guidance between the big white Station and his law firm in New York City. There, associates wearing three-piece suits carefully guided the company's many clients through the intricate mazes of corporate and personal legal actions and defenses.

Grandpa Hanson spent hours each day readying the ranch for the coming winter season, when Montana and the surrounding states would fall victim to the whims of nature, particularly the cold arctic air that would sweep down from the north.

The day-to-day operation of the Station itself was the responsibility of Grandma Hanson. Wrangler Barry saw to the livestock and ranch machinery during his visits on Sunday, Tuesday, and Thursday. He spent all his other time in classes and studies at Bozeman State University, about an hour's drive from Shadow Creek Ranch.

John and Merrilee Dawson worked long days at the homestead, building, repairing, painting, dreaming. Mr. Dawson figured it would be only a week or so before he and his wife could move their meager belongings from the Station to their new home in the mountains.

The house had been repaired and a new wood stove installed in the small living room where Wendy had spent so many hours reading through the pile of letters she'd discovered in the mirrored box. Those letters had introduced her to a little girl named

Merrilee and a grandmother who loved her dearly.

Now, 15 years since the last letter was written, Merrilee Dawson scrubbed and cleaned the home she'd only dreamed about through her correspondence with her aging grandmother.

The old woman had left the farm to Merrilee and John, a last demonstration of love from the special lady who wanted to share God's nature with the child who grew up calling her Grandmother.

Plumbing work had been contracted out earlier in the fall, and all the electrical wiring had been replaced. Repairs on some of the outbuildings had been finished, with plans to complete the rest when spring would blush the cheeks of the mountains with wildflowers.

Merrilee paused at her work and stood by the window, gazing out into the forest. "I can feel her presence," she said to her husband. "Even though she's been gone for 15 years, I can still feel her love in these rooms."

John Dawson walked to his wife's side. "I know what you mean. There's something very special about this place. I remember that whenever you'd get a letter from Mrs. Grant you'd almost sparkle. You'd open the envelope and hold the paper in your hands for a long moment before starting to read."

"I wanted to feel close to her," the woman's voice broke softly. "I knew her hands had been the last to hold that letter. I never got to see her. Not in 30 years. We couldn't afford to make the trip and she was too sick or too old to come see us. All we had were the words on those papers to show our love for each other."

John wrapped his arms around his wife. "Now you have the farm named after you. The two Merrilees are one. In your grandmother's eyes, I think they always were."

Mrs. Dawson smiled. "Thank you for agreeing to move here," she whispered. "It really feels like we're home."

The man nodded. "Yes, it does. But we'd better get back to work or our home won't be ready before the deep snows come."

"You're right," Merrilee sighed. "I'll dream and remember more when we sit by the fire and listen to the winds blowing outside. We'll have to rest up for spring. There's only enough money in our saving's account to see us through to planting time. After that, we'll have to live off the land."

"No problem," John announced with more conviction than he felt. "We're going to have beautiful gardens and cash crops. If Merrilee the farm is even half as giving as Merrilee the woman, we'll be home free. Now," the man twirled his wife around until she stood facing the chair she'd been sanding, "let's get back to work."

"Yes, sir," the woman said, throwing her husband a smart salute.

The two attacked their projects with joyful hearts. There'd be time for musing later. Just now, they had a dream to finish.

Outside, unnoticed by the busy home remodelers, the wind slowly began to shift to a more northerly direction. Animals in the forest paused in their activities and sniffed the air. Birds that had not flown south earlier perched on leafless limbs and studied the distant curves of the horizon.

An unseen force was moving across the face of the mountains and broad alpine meadows.

A squirrel chattered and flicked its tail nervously. A crow called out in a raucous voice and shook its dark feathers. Far to the northwest, a wind rose unseen, sending fingers of chill running along the rivers and streams and through the broad valleys of western Montana.

Something was about to happen—something feared by all the creatures that lived in the forests and fields surrounding Shadow Creek Ranch.

CHAPTER 2

THE LONG DARK LINE

❂   ❂   ❂

Wendy sat on the edge of her bed listening to Samantha's soft, rhythmic breathing. Dawn was just beginning to lighten the eastern sky with a faint silver glow.

Early morning was Wendy's favorite time of day. She would wander about the Station aimlessly, lost in thoughts only a 10-year-old would think. There was no one to bother her, no one to laugh or make fun, no duties to perform or schedules to keep. It was her time and hers alone.

She moved out into the long hallway of the building's south wing and ambled to the balcony that overlooked the foyer. The old clock at the base of the stairs ticked quietly, counting the seconds— endlessly, faithfully. Wendy liked the sound. To her it meant that time was passing, bringing with it new moments to savor, new challenges to face.

The young girl tip-toed down the curving stair-case and moved into the warm den where the embers of Grandpa's late-night fire still glowed in the big stone hearth.

She plopped down in her favorite chair and curled her feet up under her. Outside, beyond the big windows that lined the wide wall of the cheery room, rose majestic mountains, their summits dusted by early snows. The tall trees at the far end of the pasture stood stark and bare in the grey, early morning light. It seemed as if they'd been painted against the shadowy backdrop of mountain ranges and deep, distant valleys.

"Grandmother liked the early mornings best," a voice called from the doorway. Wendy spun around and found Merrilee standing in the warm shadows, a smile lighting her face.

"Oh, you scared me," the youngster breathed. "I wasn't expecting anyone else to be up so early."

"I'm sorry," the woman said, lifting her hand. "I didn't mean to startle you." She walked to a nearby chair and sat down quietly. "I couldn't sleep any-more. Guess I'm too excited about the farm. We're almost done. Just a few more days until we can move in."

Wendy nodded. "I think it's lookin' great. It sure isn't the way it was when Early and I found it a couple months ago." The girl chuckled shyly. "At first I thought it might be a fort with barracks and stables and stuff like that. But I'm glad it was a farm."

Merrilee smiled. "You changed our lives, Wendy Hanson. You know that, don't you?"

The girl shrugged. "I guess so. I didn't mean to. I just wanted you to know what really happened to your grandmother, that she died before she could send you her last letter." Wendy paused. "I wish I could have known her. But she was gone before I was even born."

"I think Grandma Grant would have enjoyed knowing you," the woman said. "She was so full of life, so interested in anything and everything, just like you are. You two would've made an intriguing pair."

The thought brought a grin to Wendy's face. "We could've had fun together."

Merrilee nodded. "I'm sure you would have. It's nice to have friends who are older than we are. We can learn a lot from them. They have much to teach if we'll just listen."

Wendy's smile faded. "Maybe. But some don't stay around long enough to teach you anything."

"Oh, I'm sorry," the woman urged. "I didn't mean—"

"It's OK," the girl interrupted. "I don't miss my mother, anymore. She's happy with her new husband in Connecticut and I'm happy here in Montana with everyone on Shadow Creek Ranch. Who needs her, anyway?"

Wendy stood and walked to the entrance of the den. "Besides, I'll just teach myself what I gotta know. Me and Early don't have to have some woman telling us how to act and what to do. We'll make out just fine."

With that she turned and disappeared into the foyer.

Merrilee sat for a long moment staring at the spot where Wendy had stood. She let out a long sigh and slowly laid her head against the tall back of her chair. "You're wrong, Wendy," she said quietly. "You can't do it alone. No one can."

Outside, the first ray from the rising sun pierced the eastern sky. It shot heavenward and disappeared into the vast, open canopy that spread horizon to horizon over the mountains and valleys.

Had Merrilee looked to the northwest, she would have noticed a long dark line of clouds slowly rising, as if a huge army of horse-mounted soldiers were racing down from Canada, creating a rolling, boiling cloud of black dust. In the early morning light, the shadowy line seemed to hover in the far, far distance, as if waiting for the sun to summon it south, into Montana, into the valley where Shadow Creek ran cold past frosted boulders and along ice-rimmed banks.

". . . increasing cloudiness by mid-morning as temperatures prepare to plunge." The little clock radio resting on the night stand beside Grandpa Hanson's bed rattled to life.

"A low pressure system presently situated above Alberta is expected to move southeast today, bringing with it a strong cold front that's being fed with moist air flowing east from Washington, Oregon, and Idaho."

The old man sleepily opened one eye.

"We can expect snowfall, perhaps heavy at times, east of the Divide, with accumulations of eight to 10 inches as far south as Denver during the next 24 to 48 hours.

"Montana temperatures presently range from 25 degrees in Kalispell, 31 degrees in Great Falls; Billings reports 32, and here in Bozeman it's a chilly 30 degrees. You can expect these readings to drop rapidly as the front passes over our area later today. Stay tuned to this station for hourly updates.

"Now, here with world and national news, is—"

The voice snapped into silence as the old man pressed the snooze button. He yawned broadly. After living in this part of the country for so many years, to him all weather forecasts sounded alike.

Grandpa Hanson chuckled softly to himself. Eight to 10 inches. That wasn't even worth waking up for. He pressed his cheek into the soft warm pillow. But he would mention to Tyler that it might be a good idea to dig out the tire chains. May as well be prepared when the *real* weather hit. For now, what the old man wanted most was another five minutes' sleep.

* * * * *

"Breakfast is ready!" Grandma Hanson's cheery voice echoed down the hallways and high-ceilinged rooms of the Station.

Shuffling feet and energetic voices responded from every direction as the inhabitants of the old dwelling left whatever they were doing and hurried to the big dining room. There the breakfast table waited, piled high with bowls of steaming oatmeal, plates of warm toast, and cups brimming with hot chocolate or herb tea.

After everyone had gathered, Grandpa Hanson lifted his hand and heads bowed for prayer.

"Our Father," the old man began, "thank You for this food. Thank You for healthy appetites and strong bodies to do Your bidding today.

"May we all put Your blessings to work in service for others. This we pray in Your Son's name, amen."

"Amen," the group repeated softly. Then with happy smiles everyone dove into the morning feast that Grandma Hanson and Lizzy Pierce had prepared.

After the food had disappeared and the plates were empty, save for a few crumbs, the old man at the head of the table cleared his throat. Everyone knew it was time for the day's activities to be announced. During these few moments, those around the table could encourage each other or share some suggestions. It was a time to feel part of something bigger, something important.

"I'll be driving the Dawsons up to Merrilee right after breakfast," Grandpa Hanson began, with a smile. "We might be having a little bit of snow later today and their car doesn't have chains on it as yet."

"We've got some ordered," John responded, wiping his mouth. "Should be arriving soon."

Wendy drained the last of her milk and lifted her hand. "Can I go up and help on the farm after lunch? I've got my homework for tomorrow already done."

"You do?" Lizzy queried.

"Yup," the girl nodded. "Did it this morning while you all snored in your beds."

Mr. Hanson lifted his chin. "My daughter, the genius."

Joey snickered. "We should make a new rule that all homework done before the sun comes up doesn't count."

"At least I get my assignments completed in the same month they're due," the girl mumbled, a sly grin wrinkling her face.

"Hey, I get my lessons done," the boy protested. "I just study during normal hours, like normal people."

Lizzy nodded. "Fine with me if you want to help up on Merrilee. That'll leave me some extra time to assist Joey with his history assignment."

"History." The boy said the word like it didn't taste good. "How is history going to make me a better wrangler?"

"Studying exercises another part of your body,"

Debbie giggled. She continued before Joey could respond. "This is Thursday, so I'm going into Bozeman this afternoon to work at the mall. I'll be riding in with our neighbor, Mr. Thomas. And Barry says he'll pick me up and bring me back after I'm finished. I figure around 4:30 or 5:00. He called and said he's got some stuff to get for Grandpa at the feed store, so we should be rolling in around supper time."

"Well, I'm going to go riding this afternoon," Joey asserted. "Tar Boy needs some exercise, too." He looked over at Debbie. "All parts of him."

Samantha lifted her hand.

"And you, little bit," Grandpa Hanson asked warmly. "What are your plans for today?"

"I'm going to read five books in the library, then make a cake and then build a boat."

"A boat?" the old man blinked.

"Yup. Me and Pueblo are gonna build a boat and sail to California to see all the movie stars."

"You and that dog of yours might have a little problem around Hoover Dam," Joey teased.

"That's OK. Then we'll walk or take an airplane."

Lizzy leaned down and looked into the little girl's eyes. "But we'd miss you terribly. Please don't go away."

Samantha thought for a minute. "OK," she said. "We'll just sail to Bozeman to see Debbie at the mall."

"Good," Lizzy breathed. "Besides, I wouldn't want

you to go too far away. The radio said we might have some snow."

"That reminds me," Grandpa Hanson said, lifting a finger. "The weatherman did mention the possibility of a few inches of white stuff later today. You all might want to wrap up your work a little early and get back to the Station before dark. It shouldn't be anything to worry about. But better safe than sorry, I always say."

"You never say that," Grandma Hanson chuckled.

"Well, I'm saying it now," the old man grinned.

Everyone pushed back their chairs and began the day with enthusiasm. Joey, Debbie, and Wendy headed for the den to start classes with Lizzy. Grandpa Hanson and the Dawsons left for Merrilee. Grandma Hanson attacked the piles of dirty dishes, while her lawyer son switched on his office equipment and began tapping on the computer keyboard.

Samantha dressed warmly and headed for the tool shed. She figured she'd need at least a hammer and two screwdrivers to build a boat.

* * * * *

Wrangler Barry walked quickly across the campus of Montana State University in Bozeman, on his way to the agricultural field buildings. At the moment his thoughts weren't exactly on schoolwork. He was concentrating on pipe—PVC pipe, to be exact. He and Grandpa Hanson were planning a repair job at the Station, and he had learned that a local hardware store was having a sale on sub-standard lengths of the plastic tubes. He would have to buy extra couplings, but even so it should be a good bargain.

He was just about to cross 11th Avenue and head down Lincoln Road when he happened to glance over his shoulder to the north. Looking past McCall Hall, in the direction of Bozeman, he saw a collection of dark clouds standing motionless above Bridger Range and the distant Big Belt Mountains.

The line loomed silent in the sky, as if brooding over something unpleasant. Barry noticed that the usual drift of air in and around the buildings and tennis courts on campus was gone. The air lay strangely still, unmoving, as if afraid to make itself known to the approaching specter to the north.

Look at that, the young man thought to himself, his eyes scanning the dark horizon. *Last time I saw a line like that was when I was a kid on my father's farm.*

"Hey, handsome," a female voice called from the nearby parking lot. "How 'bout helping a damsel in distress?" Barry saw an attractive coed trying to lift a bulky object from the trunk of her car. Her brown curls were jammed under a brightly colored knit cap and her cheeks glowed with youthful energy. "If I don't get this assignment to class, Professor McIntyre will flunk me for sure, and I'll have to explain to my parents that I failed college because I couldn't get a bush out of my trunk."

The wrangler laughed. "Judy," he called, hastening in the girl's direction, "you didn't have to take your assignment home with you. You could've left it in one of the field buildings like the rest of us."

"And have your yampa throwing spores all over my wake-robin? I think not!" The girl giggled, revealing two rows of straight, white teeth surrounded by naturally rosy lips. "I'll have you know this little ol' collection of plants will someday help modern woman enjoy a more painless childbirth. After all, the Indians used the rootstalks during delivery. Helped, too." She fingered a handful of delicate blossoms. "It will revolutionize medical science."

Barry pursed his lips and puffed a small stream of air. "Since when does medical science care anything about old-fashioned, Indian remedies?"

"Hey, it's becoming the in thing! They got people down in South America studying the rain forests, or what's left of them. I'll just bet that in a few years my little wake-robins will be sold as a high-priced prescription health remedy. You'll see."

Barry shrugged and looked into the friendly blue eyes laughing up at him. "Women everywhere will thank you." He lifted the carefully packed plants from the car and hoisted the bundle over his shoulder. "I hope your wake-robins help hernias, because that's what I'm going to get carrying them to class."

"Nah. For that you'll need salsify or even arrowleaf balsamroot. Helps indigestion, too." Judy smiled at her classmate as they made their way along

Lincoln Road. "Flowers and plants, especially herbs, have a lot to offer if we'd just take the time to study them carefully. I mean, animals know what to do when they get sick. They don't rush down to the local drug store."

"Lines are long enough as it is," Barry teased. "Imagine waiting for your prescription behind a bull elk with a headache."

The girl chuckled at the image Barry's words formed in her mind. "Or how 'bout a bobcat with a nervous condition?"

"Or a grizzly with acid indigestion?"

The two paused and laughed out loud, their voices bright and cheery. "Judy, you're really something," Barry said, shaking his head.

"Well, thank you, cowboy," the coed grinned. "You're really something yourself. As a matter of fact," she paused, suddenly shy, "I was wondering if you had a date for the football game this Sunday afternoon? I hear the team from Missoula isn't all that bad. Should give our guys a run for their money."

Barry cleared his throat. "Well . . . I . . . uh."

Judy gasped. "It's true. It's really true!"

"What is?" Barry asked, unsure of his classmate's strange reaction.

"You're shy," the young woman giggled. "I've heard other girls say so, but I thought they were crazy—you being so tough and manly. I thought you'd be the forward one when it came to dating."

Barry shifted the load from one shoulder to the other. "I'm not too good at all this boy-girl stuff," he said. "I feel much more comfortable around horses and crops."

Judy laughed. "Well, speaking for women everywhere, we like to think of ourselves a little bit more interesting than horses and crops."

"Oh, I'm sure you are," Barry blushed. "I've known some very interesting girls . . . I mean . . . I don't mind being around females . . . I mean . . ."

"Take it easy, cowboy," Judy giggled. "You don't have to go into any details. I just want to know if you'd like to go to the game with me. I'll try not to scare you too much."

The wrangler shrugged as best he could with the load on his shoulder. "Well, I guess so, if no emergency comes up or anything."

Judy tilted her head slightly. "What kind of emergency?"

Barry pursed his lips. "Oh, if one of the horses I'm caring for hurts itself, or comes time to foal, or whatever. Those kinds of emergencies."

"I see," Judy's grin tried to hide a giggle. "Well. Let's just hope all the animals stay nice and healthy over the weekend so we can go to the football game. OK?"

"OK," Barry nodded as Judy opened the door to one of the field buildings and let the wrangler and his burden pass by. The young man paused. "Have you ever seen a horse actually being born?" he asked. "It's really fascinating."

Judy walked down the hallway beside her enthusiastic companion, leaving the big, glass door to slowly close behind them. In the distance, the dark line had moved forward imperceptively, covering the mountain peaks with long tendrils of ash-colored clouds. The wind stirred, then died down again, as if giving second thought to its action.

* * * * *

"What time is it?" Wendy asked as she rubbed firmly on the window ledge with a soapy cloth, trying to remove another layer of dirt and grime from the pastel blue paint hiding somewhere underneath.

Merrilee looked up from her work. The doors to the kitchen cupboards all hung open, ready to receive the fresh, brightly patterned drawer paper the woman was cutting to size on the counter. "It *is* getting kinda dark," the woman said, glancing at her watch. She blinked. "Huh? That's odd. It's only quarter after three. Isn't it too dark outside for being only quarter after three?"

Wendy opened and closed her hand, trying to draw some feeling into her cramped fingers. She peered out through the window and squinted into the unusual gloom beyond the panes of clean glass.

"Yeah, it is," she agreed. "But I can't see the sky because of the trees. Grandpa did mention that we might get some snow later this afternoon or tonight.

Maybe it's just clouds drifting in."

Merrilee shrugged. "The days *are* getting shorter. Or perhaps I'm just not used to being in the mountains. Sometimes sunlight has a hard time reaching these little high-altitude valleys."

"Sure. That's all it is," Wendy reasoned. "Shorter days. A few clouds. Mountain valley. I guess I just never noticed how soon it starts to get dark up here, with winter coming. Your husband should be back soon with Grandpa's truck. Hope he remembered to get those nails we need for the upstairs floorboards. They kinda creak a lot."

"I like creaky floorboards," Merrilee said, carefully guiding her scissors along the patterned paper. "Sorta makes a house homey. Know what I mean?"

"Sorta makes a house creepy, if you ask me," Wendy retorted. "There's nothing like waking up in the middle of the night and hearing a floorboard squeak in another room, especially if you think you're the only one in the house."

The woman shivered. "Now, don't go scaring me like that. Besides, if anything," she paused, "or any*body* was wandering around uninvited in our house, John would chase him away. He's a great husband and takes very good care of me."

"I know," Wendy giggled. "I read the letters, remember?"

Merrilee smiled. "You must have thought we were kinda strange people after reviewing our lives together, at least up until 15 years ago. I had a habit of going on and on about how much we loved each other. I knew it made Grandmother happy."

"Well, you did love each other, didn't you?"

"Oh, yes," the woman beamed. "Still do. But those letters didn't contain *all* the facts. We had some rough times, too. Everyone does."

"But you had something special, right? You two were different."

Merrilee laid her scissors down and leaned against the counter. "Not really—no different than anyone else. There are things about John that I wouldn't mind terribly if he changed. And there are things about me he'd be better off not having to put up with. We both can be kinda stubborn and pigheaded. It's not easy for us to admit when we're wrong."

Wendy stopped her scrubbing and listened intently. *Stubborn. Pigheaded.* Those were words she'd heard her mother and father fling at each other late at night, when they thought she and Debbie were asleep.

"John and I decided long ago that there are things about people that can't be altered—personality traits, harmless habits that you wish the other didn't have. Those we call 'untouchables.' We don't even bother ourselves with them anymore."

Wendy's eyes opened wide. "Do you have an untouchable, Merrilee?"

The woman smiled. "Sure. Several of them."

"What are they?"

"Well," Merrilee thought for a moment, "this is one." She held up her scissors.

"Mr. Dawson doesn't like it when you cut things with scissors?"

"No," the woman laughed. "I'm just so particular about some stuff, especially the house I live in. I want it to be as perfect as it can be, so I cut out drawer liners, make the curtains just so, try to get as many things to match, colorwise, as possible. I work hard at it.

"Now, John, on the other hand, isn't so particular. He doesn't care if the drawers have liners or if the curtains match the sofa or if the bedspread shares any semblance of color with the throw rugs. To him, a house is somewhere you go to get out of the rain and eat a meal and sleep. What it looks like inside is of no consequence as far as he's concerned.

"Sometimes he gets upset with me for spending so much time trying to get things just right, or as just right as our budget will allow."

Merrilee grinned a comfortable grin. "So, he's learned that I'm not about to change my ways. That's why that part of my personality has become an 'untouchable.' He just lets me feather the nest the way I want it to be."

Wendy chuckled and looked around the room. "Would you be upset if I said I agreed with Mr. Dawson? I like pretty things; not as much as my brain-dead sister, you understand, but a house or a room is just a place to go when you can't be outside doing important stuff like riding Early or breakin' in a new gelding."

The woman nodded. "See? That's one of your untouchables. I'd know better than to pop into your bedroom down at the Station and tell you to make it just the way I want it to be. Oh, I'd insist that you sweep it once a week and keep it clean. Being sanitary is part of being healthy. But for me to tell you to pattern your room after mine just wouldn't be fair. If you wanted a burlap bedspread and feedsack curtains, then that's what you'd have, as long as they were clean."

Wendy's mouth dropped open. "That's neat. That's really neat."

"I call it 'interpersonal survival,' " Merrilee said. "Imagine what kind of world we'd have if everyone just let other people be themselves, without trying to make them conform to their own way of doing things."

The woman thought for a minute. "My grandmother used to say that's how God is with us. He has certain rules we all must follow. But then He lets us be individuals, with individual ways of doing things. She'd say in her letters, 'Merrilee, the good Lord doesn't want servants—He wants friends, brothers and sisters. That's what He wants.' I believe she was right, don't you?"

Wendy frowned. "Wait a minute. That means I have to let Debbie do what Debbie does without griping at her all the time."

"It would seem so," the woman nodded with a grin. "Sometimes it isn't easy, is it?"

Wendy shook her head, then smiled. "I like talking to you, Merrilee," she said. "You tell me neat stuff."

Mrs. Dawson wiped her forehead with the back of her hand. "But we'd better talk less and work more, right now." She looked around. "It's getting mighty dark outside. Maybe those snow clouds are gettin' here a little ahead of schedule. We'd better hurry, just in case John shows up."

The two returned to their tasks with renewed vigor. But something was very strange. The room grew darker by the minute, as if night were falling over the mountainsides and ravines. And the house seemed a little colder than before. No, not a little — much colder.

Wendy shivered and lifted her jacket from where she'd hung it earlier in the afternoon. "I hope Mr. Dawson comes soon," she said. "I have a bad feeling about this. Maybe we should be heading back to the Station right away."

* * * * *

"Debbie!" Wrangler Barry's voice echoed down the broad expanse of the almost empty Bozeman mall. "Debbie! Where are you?"

"Here I am," the girl with the long dark hair answered. As she looked over her shoulder she saw her friend running at full speed past the drygoods store. "What's the matter?"

"Come on!" Barry shouted. "We gotta go. We gotta go *right now!*"

"Why?" Debbie queried. Hurriedly she gathered her color swatches and drawing pencils and tossed them into a leather satchel. The store window would just have to wait for her to transform it into a beautiful showcase that the client would be proud of.

The wrangler was out of breath. "Don't ask any questions. We've gotta get back to Shadow Creek Ranch, and we don't have a second to spare."

"Whatever is the matter with you?" Debbie protested. "I'm not quite finished. Can't you give me another 15 minutes?"

"NO!" Barry urged. "This one's going to be bad, mark my words. If you want to get home before it hits, we have to leave this instant."

The girl began to scowl but suddenly noticed that Barry's expression wasn't just hurried; it had a look of desperation.

"Let me just say goodbye to my boss."

"OK, but hurry!" Barry called after the running girl. She soon returned and together they rushed past the deserted stores and fast-food restaurants.

"Where is everybody?" Debbie called out. "Guess I was so busy with my work that I didn't notice how empty the mall was getting."

"Haven't you been outside?" the cowboy shouted over his shoulder.

"No, not since I arrived, just after lunchtime."

The two burst through the wide entrance doors and Debbie's breath was immediately swept out of her lungs. A bone-chilling wind struck her as though she'd run into a solid wall, making her stumble and almost fall. Barry grabbed her arm to support her.

The girl's eyes opened wide. Even though it was only a little after 4:00, the sky hung dark as midnight above their heads. A fierce wind whipped across the broad parking lot, whistling past tall, swaying lamp-posts and swinging signs.

The carefully manicured trees and shrubs shivered, while crumpled newspapers and other pieces of trash blew headlong across the flat expanse of asphalt.

"What's happening?" the girl screamed, trying to be heard above the deafening roar of the wind. "Barry. WHAT'S GOING ON?"

The young man pulled harder on her arm and guided her to his big, four-wheel-drive pickup truck waiting by the curb. "Storm!" he shouted, pushing her into the roomy cab. The word was snatched from his lips and blown away.

The wrangler hurried around to the driver's side and jumped in, trying to wrest the door from the icy grip of the gale. With a heave he managed to close it.

"It's a big one, Debbie," he said breathlessly as he turned the key in the ignition. "Fasten your seatbelt tightly." He watched the tachometer spring to life, the only indication he had, in the storm's howl, that the powerful pickup's engine had started.

Jamming the vehicle into first gear, he spun the tires across the wind-swept surface of the parking lot and sped in the direction of the exit. "I should have been here earlier," he moaned, "but I wanted to get the stuff your grandfather ordered at the Co-op."

The truck roared west on Route 84. "I should've just come and picked you up." The young man's words turned to wisps of steam as he spoke. "I thought I could beat it. I should have known better. This is Montana. You don't play with the weather in Montana."

Turning south on Highway 191, Barry pushed the accelerator to the floor. The pickup lurched forward, pressing Debbie against the cool leather of her seat. "We didn't have anything so awful last winter," she said, studying the sullen sky to the south. In the distance she could make out long, wispy, dark grey arms stretching from the lower clouds to the surface of the fields that rushed past her frosted window.

"We haven't had this kind of storm for a long, long time," her companion called over the whine of the engine. "Last time was when I was a kid. Shut the whole state down for a week."

"A week?" Debbie's brown eyes shadowed with concern. "We'll make it to the ranch in time, won't we?"

"We'll sure try," Barry encouraged, pressing even harder on the accelerator. The vehicle roared past a road sign that swayed drunkenly on its pole. "If we can just beat the snow."

"I don't see any snow yet," the girl encouraged.

"Oh, really?" the wrangler shouted. "Well, what do you call that?"

He pointed behind them, to the north. Debbie leaned forward and peered into the outside mirror fastened to the passenger side of the truck. What she saw drained all color from her face.

She spun around and gazed out through the rear window and the cap that enclosed the bed of the vehicle. There, not more than five miles away and closing fast, was a huge wall of white. It rolled and tumbled like an ocean wave, driven by fierce winds. The clouds above it boiled black, illuminated from inside with jagged shafts of lightning. The white wall seemed like a wild beast of some sort, pursuing the truck down the highway.

Debbie tried to say something but the impact of what she'd seen robbed her of words. All she could do was stare at the driver, her mouth hanging open, eyes filled with terror.

"We'll make it," Barry responded to her unspoken fear, his voice not as reassuring as she wished it was. "We'll make it."

Windblown snowflakes began slapping the windshield. Debbie studied them thoughtfully. What if those little pieces of ice and water were only scouts, sent by the storm to seek out helpless travelers in the monster's path? She imagined that their job was to strike any vehicle trying to get to safety, then hurry back into the darkness behind, like worker bees returning to the hive. There they'd dance another dance—this one designed to tell the storm where the little truck and its occupants were.

"I'm scared," the girl whispered.

"What'd ya say?"

"I said I'm scared. I've never seen a storm like this."

Barry licked his lips, his mouth dry. "It's just a few more miles."

The turnoff loomed into view. "See? There's the road that will take us into the mountains, to Shadow Creek Ranch. We're almost home."

The wrangler spun the wheel and skidded his truck onto the frozen surface of the logging road that led from the highway to the ranch. "I can almost smell supper cooking," he yelled.

Suddenly, the world turned from brown and grey to white. Barry leaned forward, trying to make out the path of the gutted road as it wound through the trees and meadows. Debbie shivered as familiar forms of outcroppings and cottonwood groves became ghostlike apparitions, scowling at her through swirling masses of snow.

She was astonished at how fast the world had changed. Where earlier there had been familiar forests and glens, everything was being overwhelmingly altered by the storm. The transition from familiar to terrifying was almost instantaneous.

"It got us!" Barry shouted as he jammed the truck into four-wheel drive. The vehicle lurched as each tire suddenly found itself infused with independent power. The big wheels dug into the snow-covered surface of the road, now gripping and holding, now skidding and slipping.

"What are we going to do?" Debbie cried, her voice thick with concern.

"We're going to keep on," the driver said firmly, his lips forming a tight line across his face. "We can't turn back. Every inch we travel brings us closer to the Station."

By now, few things beyond the windshield were recognizable. Barry drove more from habit and experience than sight. He'd traversed this road hundreds of times. He could feel its curves and dips. The wrangler understood each bump and jolt as the wheels of his truck fought to maintain contact with the rugged surface of the mountain trail.

All at once, the world turned completely white. The winter monster had stretched its lethal arms over the mountains and settled on them like a predator attacking its prey. Barry drew in his breath as everything disappeared into swirling, twisting shadows.

His foot slammed the brake pedal but there was no slowing. The vehicle surged forward at an alarming speed. He didn't recognize the bumps, the jolts, the feel of the road below him.

The truck skidded sideways, completely out of

control. A grinding noise rose from underneath the pickup and the two helpless passengers felt the cab tilt violently to the right.

Debbie screamed as formless shapes rushed by, striking the metal and glass with deafening noise. Then it seemed to the pair that the bottom dropped out from below them. They felt themselves falling, falling, falling.

Barry caught a quick glimpse of something approaching at a very high rate of speed in front of the vehicle, then with a resounding crash the windshield exploded. Snow, ice, and glass struck the pair like a shotgun blast. Finally all was silent, still, unmoving.

Above, the wind howled and shrieked, as if somewhere someone was laughing, the voice echoing in the thunder. Barry watched as his world turned grey, then black. Sinking into unconsciousness, he heard himself cry, "Debbie. DEBBIE!"

There was no response.

CHAPTER 3

MONSTER

❂ ❂ ❂

Joey stared at the sky with unbelieving eyes. He was sitting astride Tar Boy in the far pasture, beyond the cottonwoods, where Grandpa Hanson and Barry had cleared the land in preparation for spring planting.

"Look at that," the boy said to his big, black horse. "I've never seen that kind of clouds before. Must be a storm, and I think it's comin' this way."

The animal sniffed the air, then blew a fine mist of steam from his broad nostrils. He shook his head and snorted again, nervously.

"I agree," Joey nodded, as if in response to Tar Boy's unspoken suggestion. "We'd better get back to the corral *fast!*"

The boiling band of clouds and snow bore down

from the northwest with fearsome speed. As the horse and rider raced along the curving driveway that led from the logging road to the big house by the creek, Joey felt sharp pellets of ice begin to sting his face. He urged the animal to even greater haste and squinted against the tiny obstacles that filled the air. "What's going on?" he called. "Storms don't move this fast."

As the two crossed the footbridge, the world suddenly turned white. In seconds the ground was covered with a thickening shroud of snow and the air turned bone-chilling cold.

Tar Boy skidded to a stop and rose on his powerful hind legs, fanning the gusting winds with his hooves. "Come on," Joey urged, his voice thin and trembling, fear tugging at his heart. "Come on, Tar Boy. We gotta get to the corral."

The young wrangler dug his heels into the horse's flanks and tried to steer his steed in the general direction of the horse barn that waited beyond the tack shed. He could catch only quick glimpses of the structure through the blinding snows. In one movement Joey slid to the ground. The horse snorted and sidestepped, yanking on the leather straps that the determined boy held as he led him along.

"Get in there, Tar Boy!" Joey screamed, trying to be heard above the sudden gale. He slapped the big animal's rump with the loose ends of the reigns. "Get in there now!"

The big stallion impatiently followed his leader

into the enclosure and paced back and forth as Joey tried to wrestle the broad, wooden door closed behind them. It took a mighty shove to slam the portal shut. Snowflakes that had been driven by the howling wind outside suddenly found themselves in a calmer atmosphere and floated daintily to the straw-covered floor.

"MAN!" Joey gasped, leaning against a pile of feed sacks to catch his breath. "What's goin' on? I ain't never seen a storm come up so fast!"

The stallion stomped his hooves and tossed his mane back and forth, eyes wide with terror, ears flattened against the top of his noble head.

A sudden bang on the barn door made Joey jump. He spun around and hurried to the entrance. Leaning against the gale, he forced the door open again. Before he could get out of the way, Early burst into the barn, followed by several other terrified horses. The boy sprawled across the straw, sending clouds of dust swirling in the frigid air.

"Well, come on in," he called, rubbing his elbow. "Don't wait for an invitation." Joey stumbled to his feet. "OK, OK. Let's see, one, two, three, four, five. Yup. Everybody's here."

He hurried back to the door and wrestled it shut, his teeth clenched against the powerful force of the wind. "Good thing we don't keep any more riding horses on the ranch during the winter. There wouldn't be enough room in the barn."

The animals milled about in anxious confusion.

"Settle down, critters," the boy called, trying to sound soothing. "It's just a little ol' storm. We'll wait it out. Haven't you learned that Montana blows make a big noise at first, then settle into your normal, everyday brand of blizzard? In a half hour or so, I'll head over to the Station and leave you guys here to enjoy all this grain and oats. Tough life you beasts live. Real tough."

Tar Boy pressed close to his master, nervously eyeing the closed barn door. "Now, everyone get into your stalls and settle down. Go on, Tar Boy. Move it, Early." Joey pushed against the smooth flanks of the animals. "You too, Sapphire. Come on, White Star. And get off my foot, Pookie." The boy paused. "Why Grandpa Hanson let Samantha name you Pookie is more than I know. That's a stupid name for a horse." He paused again. " 'Course, you're a stupid horse, so maybe that's OK."

The small, dappled animal turned and stared at the boy. "Oh, all right. Maybe you ain't stupid, but that's still the craziest name for a horse I ever heard. Pookie. Sounds like something a rich lady would call her dog."

With a little more urging, all the animals finally took their assigned places in the comfortable barn. Joey scooped oats from the feed bin by the work table and gave a generous portion to each of his four-footed charges. He tried to ignore the rattling, shaking walls that surrounded them.

"Some wind, huh?" he said, trying to keep his

own mind occupied, the sound of the gale making him uncomfortable. "Well, you're all safe and sound in here. This old barn's been around for at least a hundred years. Maybe more. When this ranch was a way station, folks on their way to Yellowstone used to bed down their horses in here, you know, the ones pullin' the wagons and fancy buggies. You guys are lucky. You're just ridin' horses. Man, I tell you, it weren't easy being a horse a hundred years ago. No, sir."

The boy walked to the far wall and tried to peer through the wooden slats. Seeing nothing, he carefully pressed the door open a few inches. A blast of frigid air followed by spraying snow hit him hard across the face. He blinked and coughed while quickly relatching the broad portal. "Maybe I'll just wait in here with you," he said to the animals who now were contentedly munching on their oats. "Doesn't look too friendly out there right now."

Joey sat down and leaned his head against the feed sacks. He frowned. What was going on outside the sturdy walls of the horse barn? He'd seen snows, and he'd seen storms. But this? If it kept up any longer, he was going to start getting concerned.

The boy picked up a piece of straw and twirled it in his fingers. "Don't worry," he said aloud. "It'll be over soon. I'll be back in the Station before supper."

* * * * *

The leading edge of the blizzard hit the little farm

in the mountains like a giant fist. Wendy had just returned to the house with an armload of wood for the stove when she felt the air turn suddenly chill.

As she walked toward the open door it slammed shut, driven by a gale-force gust that bent the trees and rattled the rafters. It felt as if the building was in the jaws of an angry dog.

The lighted candles on the newly painted kitchen table flickered out, leaving the room in almost total darkness.

Merrilee was upstairs in the bedroom putting the finishing touches on her wallpaper when a large limb smashed through the window and impaled itself into the chest of drawers like an out-of-control bulldozer.

She screamed as a seemingly solid mass of icy air struck her broadside, knocking her to the floor. Hail the size of golf balls pounded the tin roof of the farmhouse with deafening resonance.

"Wendy!" the woman cried out. "Wendy, are you all right?"

The young girl appeared at the door, face pale, eyes wide with terror. "Are we going to die?" she shrieked. "Are we going to die?"

Merrilee jumped up and pushed the girl into the hallway, slamming shut the bedroom door behind her. Together they slipped to the floor and huddled in the darkness at the top of the stairs. It seemed that nothing around them would survive. They heard wood splintering and snapping, and glass breaking. Downstairs, pots and pans that had been neatly stored in the cupboards rattled and banged to the floor. The building strained on its foundation.

"Oh, dear God! Oh, dear God!" Merrilee called out, holding Wendy close to her. "Help us. SAVE US!"

Her words were lost in the roar of the wind.

* * * * *

"The shutters! Close the shutters!" Grandpa Hanson and John Dawson raced across the broad foyer of the Station and into the den. The big wooden shutters designed to protect the windows from wind and rain were quickly latched, sealing the room in darkness.

"I've got to get up to Merrilee," the younger man urged. "May I borrow your farm truck? It should have pretty good traction."

"Not on your life," Grandpa Hanson shouted over the roar of the wind. "You won't get a hundred yards out there."

"But what are we going to do? They'll be stuck up there in an unfinished house." He paled. "I've got to try."

"NO!" the old man persisted. "You won't make it. I can't let you go. It's best to be either here at the Station or there on the farm, not somewhere in between. Listen to that wind. It's not fooling around. It means business."

Mr. Dawson groaned. "Oh, why didn't I leave an hour ago? I spent too much time working on that new bedframe."

"Look, John," Grandpa Hanson called, straining to latch the fluttering shutter while powdery snow blew hard against his face. "If you'd gone when you'd planned, you all might have been caught out on the logging road. Believe me, you, your wife, and Wendy are a whole lot better off right where you are."

"I suppose you're right," the younger man agreed hesitantly. "I just wish they were here with us in the Station."

Grandpa Hanson smiled. "They'll be all right. We have to leave them in God's hands for a little while." The wind rattled the shutters and knocked a plant from the window box. "I guess we're *all* in God's hands right now," the old man continued. "I've never seen anything like this, not ever."

Throughout the old structure, hurried hands labored, trying to protect the house from the wrath of the storm.

Lizzy locked all the entrance doors on the lower level, then hurried from room to room, making sure windows were closed and shutters latched.

The building moaned almost humanlike as fierce winds pounded its age-old face and broad sides. It had survived other storms, but this one seemed somehow different: angry, mean-spirited, bent on destruction.

"Is it going to crash down on us?" a little girl's thin, fear-filled voice echoed along the upstairs hallway. "Is the storm going to make us fly away?"

Samantha ran along behind Grandma Hanson,

trying to find reassurance from the worried adults who rushed past her, each on an urgent errand. "What if the wall breaks? What if the roof breaks? Is it going to hurt bad?"

The old woman paused and caught the girl in her arms. "Oh, no," she said. "Everything's going to be OK, Sam." Grandma Hanson smiled in the dim light. "We just have to prepare the Station so it will be strong and protect us."

"Oh," the little girl breathed. "So we're not going to fly away and get hurt real bad?"

"No, no," Grandma Hanson said, passing her fingers through the youngster's tightly curled locks. "We're just going to finish our work, then wait for the winds to die down. Would you like to help?"

Samantha brightened. "Yeah. What do you want me to do?"

"Go find Pueblo and take him to the den where you'll both be safe. OK?"

The girl spun around and headed down the long passageway. "Here, Pueblo. Here, Pueblo," Grandma Hanson heard her call. The woman rose and ran to her son's office.

"Tyler," she called as she entered the room. "Everything all right in here?"

The lawyer looked up from his desk. "I've got my data saved and equipment turned off. I was just about to start unplugging stuff. If there's any lightning in this monster storm, it could fry all my computer circuits in a heartbeat. Do the phones still work?"

"I think so," Grandma Hanson called over her shoulder as she headed for one of the two curving staircases. "Make sure your windows are latched and the shutters in place. I'm going to check and see how your father's doing downstairs."

The man nodded and reached for the telephone.

Grandpa Hanson was just coming out of the kitchen when he saw his wife passing by the entrance to the dining room. "Have you seen Joey?" he called.

The woman stopped. "No, as a matter of fact, I haven't."

Grandpa Hanson closed his eyes and tilted his head back a little. "I think he was out riding."

"Oh, my," his wife breathed. "You don't suppose—"

"Joey's a smart kid," he reasoned. "He'd know to head for the corral—that is, if he had enough time."

"I seen Joey," Samantha called from under the table. She emerged with a frightened dog held tightly in her arms. "He and Tar Boy were going across the bridge when everything went white and the wind made me scared."

"Praise the Lord!" the old man shouted.

"Praise the Lord!" Samantha repeated, a happy smile spreading across her face.

Grandma Hanson bent and gave the diminutive dog-catcher a hug. "Then I'm sure he made it to the barn. Even if the snow blinded him, Tar Boy would get them there. Horses can track through anything."

"You're right," the old man agreed. "I think we can safely assume that Joey's in the barn. But there's one way to be sure." He ran to the den and grabbed the ranch's small walkie-talkie from the mantle. "Wrangler Barry keeps a receiver charging beside his cot. If Joey is out there, he'll hear our call."

* * * * *

Tar Boy shifted his weight from one hoof to another as he watched his human friend pacing back and forth in front of his stall.

"I'm beginning to get worried," the boy was saying. "I mean, what if this storm lasts for days and days? I might be stuck out here with you guys 'til I'm old and gray. Spring will come and they'll find me, frozen like a snow cone, propped up by the feed sacks." He turned. "What do you think, Early? How long is this storm going to last?"

"Joey, can you hear me?" A voice sounded from the far end of the barn.

The boy stiffened and looked closely at Wendy's horse. "Did you say something?" He listened, then shook his head vigorously. "Must be the wind."

"Hey, Joey, can you hear me?"

"Wait a minute," the youngster said, scratching his head. "The wind doesn't know my name."

"Come on, Joey, if you can hear me, answer."

The young wrangler blinked his eyes. "Man, I'm

going crazy. I swear the wind is callin' me." He frowned. "Oh, sure. It probably wants me to waltz outside and play with it. It's teasing me, that's what's happenin'. It's trying to get me to leave this warm, yet smelly, horse house and go stumbling around outside. Well, no way."

The boy lifted his chin. "I'll just stay here, thank you very much. After all, I've got a roof over my head, at least for now, and blankets over there, a cot, a walkie-talkie on the shelf, a—"

Joey gasped. "A walkie-talkie!" He rushed across the room. "That's what I heard. I wondered how come the wind sounded so much like Grandpa Hanson."

The boy grabbed the little communication device and pressed the transmit button. "Hey, Grandpa, is that you callin' me?"

"Are you all right, son?" the electronic voice queried. Even above the roar of the wind, Joey could hear relief in the old man's words.

"Yeah, I'm just fine, considerin'. Is this a storm or what?"

"Listen, Joey," the voice urged, "you've got to prepare for cold. Do you hear me? You've got to get the barn as ready as possible for the night hours. Temperatures are going to drop way, way down. Over."

"How do I do that?"

Grandpa's directions crackled with the sound of thunder overhead. "Fill in as many cracks in the

walls as you can. Use straw or cloth or whatever.
You've got to keep the wind out and body warmth in.
How many horses are with you?"

"All of 'em," Joey called, his finger pressing hard
on the transmit button. "Over."

"Great! That's terrific! You'll be able to keep each
other from freezing. Don't even think of starting a
fire in there because you might burn the place down,
so just seal the cracks and wrap up in as many
blankets as you can find. Over."

"OK," the boy said, looking around. "Don't worry
about us." He paused. "Are Wendy and Mrs. Dawson
still at Merrilee?"

"I'm afraid so," the disembodied voiced replied.
"Over."

Joey pressed the transmit button. "How 'bout
Debbie and Barry?"

Grandpa was about to respond when he looked
up and saw his son entering the den. "I've just been
on the phone with Bozeman," the young lawyer
announced slowly. "The mall security guard said he
saw Debbie and Barry leave about two and a half
hours ago." Mr. Hanson sat down on the sofa. "The
police have closed the interstate because of snow
and high winds. They said all roads have become
impassible across the entire southern portion of the
state."

He looked at his parents, his eyes revealing the
deep fear in his heart. "That means my little girl is

out there in this storm somewhere between here and Bozeman."

"She'll be OK, Tyler," Grandma Hanson said softly. "Wrangler Barry will—"

"That's not all," the man interrupted. "The security guard said the latest weather forecast says we can expect more than eight *feet* of snow. It's being called the storm of the century, and it's only two hours old."

Mr. Hanson rose slowly and walked to the foyer. "I'll be in my office," he called without turning. The stunned group watched him climb the steps and disappear from view.

"Joey?" the old man called, the walkie-talkie still at his ear.

"I heard, Grandpa Hanson," Joey's voice rattled in the device. "I heard what he said."

* * * * *

The meadow bustled with activity. Dazzling wildflowers bloomed in broad expanses of velvet grasses, and squirrels played among the low-hanging branches moving with the gentle breeze. Birds soared in the azure sky, their songs filling the air.

"I found one," a child's voice called out. "Come see, Daddy. I've found one."

Tiny fingers wrapped around the delicate blossoms. "See? It's a beautiful wake-robin. Can I take it home? Can I?"

The child glanced up. The meadow had suddenly

become all white. The trees were gone. There was nothing but a flat expanse of powdery snowdrifts cresting like ocean waves along a beach; rolling, rolling, rolling.

"Where are the flowers?" the little voice called. "Where did they go?"

The boy gasped. The waves in the meadow grew higher and higher. The sky had turned black. He felt something between his fingers. He looked down. The wake-robin blossom had become an ugly, twisted piece of metal, hot to the touch. He dropped it and the object shattered against the white ground, setting the snow on fire.

"Daddy!" the little boy screamed. "It's hot. The fire is hot!"

Above him the waves continued to build until he couldn't see the sky. He jumped up and started to run across the meadow, the bottoms of his feet burning. "*No!*" he shouted. "Go away, fire. Go away, snow. Leave me alone."

The giant wave crested and started falling toward him. He couldn't move. The fire grew hotter. The wave kept falling. He was trapped—trapped between fire and ice.

"*No!*" he heard someone calling. "*No!*"

Barry's eyes opened. Who was shouting? He listened. Wait. It was he. He was the little boy. He was shouting. The white wave descended with a crushing blow.

The wrangler stiffened, pain stabbing his chest.

He wasn't in a meadow. He was somewhere else. Somewhere dark. Somewhere silent and cold.

Slowly he began to remember. The winding road. The racing truck. The snow. So much snow. Couldn't see. Couldn't see the road! Falling. *Falling!*

"*No,*" Barry cried out, his breath labored. "*No!*"

The dream faltered, then faded away in the thick darkness.

Slowly, ever so slowly, the odd-shaped forms surrounding him began to take on recognizable designs. He saw the steering wheel, bent and twisted against the dashboard, compressed by the impact of his own body. Beside him were sacks of grain, thrown forward into the cab of the truck by the wrenching crash. One sack had a large gash in its side. A steady stream of grain flowed from the open wound. The kernels tumbled past a crumpled box of leather straps and through the still, white fingers of a hand that jutted from the pile.

He studied the fingers for a long moment. How strange they looked. How very strange. They weren't his, that was for sure. His fingers weren't that dainty, that smooth. His were rough, work-worn, weathered by the sun and seasons.

But those fingers were gentle, curved so artistically.

The horseman closed his eyes, fighting the painful haze that tried to creep over him. He must stay awake. He mustn't dream again.

Why? He wasn't sure. His work was done. Was

there something else he was supposed to do today? Barry fought to remember. He'd finished his classes on time. Just as he'd promised, he'd stopped at the mall and picked up Debbie. Hadn't he taken her back to the Station, back to Shadow Creek Ranch?

No. Wait. Now he remembered. There was a storm. Yes. A storm. He was driving fast. Very fast. But the storm was chasing him. He couldn't outrun it. It kept coming. And coming. *And coming!*

"We'll make it," he called out loud, his voice choked. "Don't worry, Debbie. We'll m—"

Barry gasped. Debbie? Yes. Debbie was with him when he crashed. He began to tremble as he studied the hand jutting from the feed sacks. Oh, no! That was Debbie's hand.

He reached out and closed his fingers around the pale palm. It was cold, like the air in the cab.

"Debbie?" he whispered, the word sounding thick, unnatural. "Debbie, can you hear me? Please, can you hear me?"

He waited as full realization of what had happened took form in his mind. "Please answer, Debbie," he begged. "Oh, please be OK."

He felt the hand move slightly, and a moan escaped from unseen lips.

"DEBBIE!" he shouted. "CAN YOU HEAR ME?"

"What . . . what happened?" a thin, high voice spoke hesitantly from beyond the tangled collection of sacks and supplies.

Relief flooded the horseman's body as he heard

the words. She wasn't dead. At least he knew that much. But how badly was she hurt?

"We had an accident," he said. "We slipped off the road." The wrangler looked around, trying to get his bearings. "I can't see anything outside and I don't know why."

Suddenly, the truth struck him hard, forcing the air from his lungs.

"Oh my!" he breathed, unbelieving.

"What is it?" the voice asked.

"We're . . . we're buried under the snow, Debbie!" he said. "Do you hear me? We've been completely buried by the storm."

Barry waited in the dim darkness of the cab. The only illumination seemed to be coming from somewhere outside. But where? He glanced down at the controls behind the smashed steering column. Of course. The headlights.

He reached down and pressed a lever. The world went completely black.

"Barry?" the weak voice called. "Will they find us?"

The young man leaned his head against the cool glass by his ear. "That depends."

"On what?"

The wrangler closed his eyes, a burning fear pressing against him like fire. "The storm," he said. "That depends on the storm."

High above, unseen by the two occupants of the buried truck, the monster roared, its icy breath screaming through the trees and howling over mountain tops. Snowdrifts formed cresting waves across the meadows, covering the face of the land with a heavy mask of white.

Night had fallen. Southern Montana lay trapped under the speeding blizzard's tread.

CHAPTER 4

NIGHT WINDS

❋ ❋ ❋

Wendy sat cross-legged in front of the wood-burning stove, trying to coax flames from the partially dried logs stacked neatly inside.

She'd carefully crumpled up some paper plates found in the trash bin. They'd been tossed there a couple days earlier, after the group had enjoyed a pizza feast. For some reason, no one had bothered to take the trash down to the Station.

Outside, in the darkness, the wind whistled through the forest, sounding not so much like a storm as like a speeding train.

Every few seconds, a window would rattle or a loose board would squeak somewhere in the little two-story farmhouse. Wendy tried her best to ignore the strange noises, concentrating instead on getting the fire going.

Even if and when she did, the girl knew that they had only one armload of wood to warm themselves with. Somehow, they'd have to get more fuel, and soon. The only supply of logs was neatly stacked out in the shed, 30 feet from the front door. Usually this would not be a problem. But just now there happened to be a blizzard between her and the woodpile.

"I'm trying to light wet wood with damp paper plates," she mumbled as she struck another match and held the tiny flame against the singed corner of a brightly-colored platter. "Where's a good flamethrower when you need one?"

Merrilee chuckled and looked up from the kitchen table where she was trying to open a can of baked beans with a pair of pliers. "We weren't exactly prepared for this, were we?" she sighed. "I don't remember inviting this storm into our state, do you?"

Wendy nodded. "Squall line. That's what it's called."

"I beg your pardon?"

The youngster struck another match and held it to the plate. "Squall line. That's the leading edge of a cold front that has lots of wind and hail. I learned about it in a book I read about flying."

"Is that what hit us?"

"Yup. The squall line comes first and then the main portion of the storm. If you're a pilot, you keep away from fast-moving cold fronts or you'll crash and burn."

"Oh, dear," Merrilee gasped. "Sounds awful." She rotated the can in her hand and took another grip with the pliers. "Do you want to be a pilot when you're older?"

"Maybe," Wendy responded, watching a thin wisp of smoke curl from the dark circle of burned paper. "I haven't decided yet."

The woman at the table gave her pliers a firm squeeze. "Well, I don't like squall lines or storms or cold fronts or tin cans that won't open."

"I wasn't scared," the girl announced. "I just went upstairs to make sure you were OK."

"Thank you," Merrilee smiled, glancing at her companion then back at the can of beans. "You were a great comfort. I thought the house would blow away."

"Nah. It's a tough ol' building. And our hard work has made it even tougher. No storm is going to knock it down. No, sir." The girl paused. "Even Mr. Underfoot knows that. He's probably in the attic rolled up in a ball, hibernating. He feels safe here."

A tiny flame flickered, then began to grow. "All right!" Wendy enthused. "One warm, crackling fire comin' up."

"Good going, Wendy!" Merrilee responded with a shout. "And I've about got supper ready. Hope you like baked beans. John and I found them on sale in Bozeman. Bought a whole case. I'm afraid that's all we've got to eat until someone rescues us."

The girl held a piece of kindling to the flame. "Right now, I'm hungry enough to eat one of these logs."

Tomato sauce squirted from the jagged hole in the can and sprayed Merrilee in the face. She cried out in frustration. "Remind me to bring a can opener up here our very next trip from the Station."

Wendy giggled. "Isn't the food supposed to go in your mouth?"

Merrilee picked up a dust rag and wiped her forehead. "My mother use to say that when I was a little girl I always insisted on *wearing* my supper. Said mashed potatoes were my favorite. I heard her tell her friends that I could turn into an Idaho spud right before her eyes." The woman smiled. "Mealtime and bathtime were the same when I was a child."

Wendy giggled. "Samantha sort of wears her food from time to time, too. Joey says her mouth is always too busy talking."

Logs crackled and hissed as moisture battled flame within the confines of the new stove set in the corner by the living room window.

"Joey's a pretty nice fellow," Merrilee said, forcing the can's lid open and pouring its contents into two cooking pots. "Your father told us the story of how you all came out from New York. Exciting stuff."

"Yeah. He's OK, for a boy. He's learning horses pretty good. Wrangler Barry said he never saw anybody work so hard to learn the horse business in all his life."

"That's because it's important to him," the woman said, seating herself on the floor beside Wendy. "People always work hard at things they consider important." She handed her companion a small pot of baked beans. "This house is important to John and me, so we don't even think of what we're doing here as work. It's fulfilling a dream."

Wendy nodded slowly. "I kinda thought it would be. You talked about lots of dreams in your letters to your grandmother. Are you sad most of them didn't come true?"

The woman shook her head. "Dreams are funny things. They change as the years roll by. I guess reality makes it so. That's when you create new dreams, new wishes."

"Well," Wendy sighed, looking down at her pile of beans, "right now I wish I had a spoon to eat my supper with."

Merrilee laughed. "That's why God gave us fingers, so that if we were ever caught in a blizzard with nothing to eat but beans, and no spoons in sight, we'd survive just fine until someone came and rescued us . . . or brought us some silverware." The woman took in a deep breath. "And speaking of God, maybe we'd better bow our heads and thank Him for keeping the house standing for another day and, hopefully, for at least another night."

Wendy grinned and closed her eyes. "Our Father," she prayed, "thank You for keeping us safe until now. Thank You for these beans. And be with everyone down at the Station. Help us to figure out how to get that wood out of the shed before we freeze to death and die. In Jesus name, amen."

"Amen," Merrilee whispered.

The fire crackled in the stove, its warmth pressing in on the two diners seated before it. "Next time," the woman announced, "we'll have *hot* baked beans."

"Not *too* hot," Wendy giggled, holding up her sauce-covered fingers.

"Oh yeah. No spoons." The two fell silent as they hungrily devoured the sweet tasting legumes. Outside, the wind continued to howl and the snow fell deeper and deeper against the old homestead.

* * * * *

Joey studied the windward wall of the corral, eyeing the clusters of straw stuck between boards here and there. He shivered a little and pulled the saddle blanket he was wearing tighter around his chin.

"That's almost got it," he called to his four-legged companions. "You guys see any more holes anywhere?"

The horses snorted and stomped their hooves contentedly. "Oh sure, you don't care," the boy quipped. "You're used to being out here in the cold. Well, I ain't. This is not my idea of home sweet home.

I'm hungry. I'm tired. And I'm cold. Not a good combination."

Tar Boy shook his head, his long mane flowing in the frigid damp air. "Yeah, I know," the boy nodded. "I'm not a horse. Thanks for recognizing that fact. I should be in the Station sitting by the fire, eating Grandma Hanson's stew." Joey paused. "Oh, why did I think of her stew! I'll go crazy if I imagine food, especially Grandma Hanson's vegetable stew."

He paced back and forth across the floor. "Why didn't Barry leave any food out here? He slept in the barn all summer. Didn't the guy ever get hungry for some snacks or anything? Why'd we have to hire a healthy wrangler? You'd think he would have stashed some corn chips under his cot, or a bag of candy behind the tools, like normal people."

Joey flopped down on the cot and covered his feet with his blanket. He watched the candle glow on the workbench, its flickering light casting long shadows on the walls. "What I wouldn't give right now for a piece of Lizzy's cornbread just dripping with honey. I'd wash it down with a cold glass of milk." He blinked. "What am I saying? Forget the cold milk. Make that hot milk. Or better yet, hot chocolate. And forget the cornbread and make that soup. Hot soup. Hot stew. Yeah, Grandma Hanson's delicious hot stew."

The boy jumped to his feet. "Aaah! I did it again! I thought about stew. Man, I've gotta stop doin' that." He began pacing back and forth once more. "They're gonna find a frozen *skinny* snow cone in here in the spring." He grabbed the walkie-talkie. "Hey, Grandpa Hanson, you hear me?"

There was a long pause. Then, "Yeah, Joey. How you doin' out there?"

"Terrible."

Grandpa Hanson's voice sounded concerned. "What's the matter? Are you too cold?"

Joey shook his head. "No, I'm OK there. I'm hungry. I keep thinking about Grandma Hanson's vegetable stew and it's driving me bonkers."

He heard the old man chuckle. "I'm sorry, Joey. There's no way we can get food out to you right now. The snow is up to the downstairs windows all around the Station. We can't see more than 10 feet from the house. And five minutes ago we lost power. It's going to be a long night. Over."

Joey sighed. "I just wish there was something to eat around here. I mean anything. I've even considered munching on the horse feed. Over."

"Why don't you?" came the quick reply. "Just take it easy, eat a little at a time, and chew it up good. Over."

The boy shrugged. "I guess I could. I ain't never ate horse food before."

"Sure you have. Only we call it breakfast cereal. Difference is, one's cooked, one's raw."

"Well, if you think it's OK, I guess I'll give it a try. Over and out."

Joey walked to the feed bin and stared at the piles

of wheat stored there. He reached down and picked up a few kernels and held them in his hand. Slowly, he placed them in his mouth and began to chew. He chewed and chewed and chewed and chewed. After what seemed a very long time, he swallowed. Glancing over at the horses standing in their stalls watching him, he smiled weakly. "Needs salt," he said.

* * * * *

Snow swirled above the high banks, forming random patterns across the road and drifting into the deep ravine to one side. There were no traces of anything living except for gnarled, leafless tree branches that occasionally broke the surface of the drifts.

The only indication that a vehicle may have recently passed by were a few broken limbs hanging from the wind-blown trees that guarded the edge of the roadway.

The night moaned like a dying animal as the face of the land sank deeper and deeper under a blanket of white.

Beneath the snow, down in the ravine where a brook used to sing its summer song, Barry's truck lay smothered by the storm. Its front end pointed slightly upward; the frame tilted to the right just a little.

Inside the cab, there was movement.

"Hang in there, Debbie," the wrangler encouraged as he pulled another sack of feed through the shattered back window and let it drop into the covered truck bed. "I've got to check you out. Make sure nothing's broken."

The girl felt the weight that pressed on her shoulders and left side ease little by little as the young man worked to shift the load off his passenger. She nodded in the darkness. "How can you see what you're doing?"

"Flashlight," she heard the wrangler say. "And I've got a first-aid kit in the glove compartment and some other stuff back here. Just as soon as I get you out from under the supplies, I've got to get a line of this PVC pipe up to the surface of the snow. Grandpa Hanson had me pick some up. We're doing some work on the waterlines in the Station."

"You gonna try to call for help?"

"No," the young man chuckled painfully, his chest and sides aching with the strain. "Oxygen. Gotta get some air down here."

Debbie shifted in her seat. "Are we going to freeze to death?"

"I don't think so," her companion replied. "Snow is a good insulator. Just ask the Eskimos. They build houses out of the stuff. We just have to get a constant supply of oxygen into the truck. I think I can do it, depending on how hard the snow is packed. My guess is, not all that hard. Not yet, anyway."

The teenager felt the bag at her back and neck slowly ease away. "Well, hello, young lady," she heard Barry say as a beam of light played on the icy window by her head. "You come here often?"

She grinned slightly. "Not if I can help it."

Barry lifted more bags until none were left in the cab. He carefully arranged the feed sacks in the back of the truck, then appeared at the rear window. "So, can you move everything? Fingers? Toes? Arms?"

Debbie gently exercised her limbs. "Ouch. My shoulder hurts pretty bad."

Barry nodded. "Well, I should think so. You had a two-weeks' supply of oats come in through this window trying to bury you alive. Just make sure nothing's broken. Stiff is OK. Sore is OK. Broken is *not* OK."

The girl flexed her legs and arms. She slowly moved her head forward, then back. "I think I'm still in one piece. Just a little cold."

Barry disappeared then reappeared, a thick blanket in his hand. "Here, spread this over you. Oh, and you can take your seatbelt off. I don't think we're moving fast enough to need it."

Debbie unfastened the chromed latch in her lap and the belt clanked to the floor. "Now just sit quietly," Barry directed, "and I'll get working on the air vent. You still may be hurt and not know it, so just take it easy."

The young man grimaced as he moved back to the rear of the truck bed. "Barry! You're hurt," Debbie called. She grabbed the rearview mirror and quickly adjusted it until she could see her companion's dimly lit form in the back. "Let me help you."

"I'm OK," Barry called. "I think I might have a few cracked ribs or something. Stupid me. Didn't put on my shoulder harness, just the seatbelt. Glad they build collapsible steering columns into these newer trucks or I'd be a shish-ka-bob right about now."

Debbie shivered as she looked at the steering wheel pushed flat against the dashboard. "Mark one up for modern technology," she said.

"You got that right. Now where did those plastic pipes get to? Everything's a mess back here. Grandpa had me pick up a bunch of supplies at the Co-op. I even got some groceries at the store for your grandmother. Are you hungry?"

"No," the girl responded. "Just get us some air down here. It's beginning to get a little stuffy."

The wrangler nodded and gathered several pieces of three-inch-diameter pipe. He was glad now they were not the standard 10 feet in length; several were not more than five.

He pushed at the Plexiglas window at the rear of the pickup cap, but the window wouldn't budge. "Guess I'll have to use the driver-side opening in the cab," he called. "I'll put a cap on this first pipe and use it to bore up to the surface. Here goes."

Debbie watched as Barry wrestled the pipe from behind her and pushed it up through the snow at the "upper" side of the cab. Twisting the tube back and forth, he carefully guided it up, up, up through the drifts.

When most of the first length had disappeared he

joined a second to it with a coupling—no need for glue. This, too, he slowly worked up through the cold, icy mass.

As the third length was about halfway up into the snow, Barry felt the resistance slacken. "That's it. We're at the top." He whistled softly to himself. "There's about 12 feet of snow between us and the storm. And that could become even more. I'll make sure we have plenty of extra tubing up there."

He pulled the pieces back into the truck, separating them carefully, one by one. From the last length to come down, he worked off the cap. Then, working quickly, he reversed the action, pushing the pipe back up through the hole, this time without the cap. As the top section cleared the surface of the snow he could feel a current of cold air blowing from the pipe in his hand. He and Debbie could also hear the echoed sounds of the storm. They sat in silence, listening to the roar as it passed down the length of the plastic tubing.

"Sounds kinda bad," Barry said somberly. "This may be an unusual statement, but I'd rather be down here in the truck than up there in all that wind."

Debbie turned her face as tears moistened her eyes. The wrangler reached through the window and placed his hand on her shoulder. "We'll be OK, Debbie. I promise. They'll come looking for us as soon as they can."

The girl nodded. "But how will they find us? We're 12 feet under the snow. And no one has any

84

idea where we are, to begin with."

Barry searched in his jacket pocket for his handkerchief. "I'll get us out of here," he said softly. "I promise."

He was about to pass the cloth to his companion when he began to cough. He held the handkerchief to his own mouth and bent double in the darkness, his chest searing with pain. It felt like hot knives were stabbing him over and over again. He fell backward into the truck bed, his face contorted with agony.

"Barry!" Debbie screamed, quickly turning and wiggling through the opening between the cab and the truck bed. "What's the matter? You're hurt, aren't you? You're hurt bad."

She picked up the fallen flashlight and shone it on her friend's face. Barry's hand dropped from his mouth, still clutching the handkerchief. The white cloth was stained with bright, red blood.

* * * * *

Tyler Hanson sat unmoving at the end of his bed. A single candle, resting on the nightstand beside an open Bible, illuminated the lawyer's face with soft yellow light and threw his shadow, large and dark, against the far wall.

Outside, the storm howled, occasionally rattling the tightly closed shutters that guarded the room's only window from nature's rage.

The man's eyes were closed, as if he were trying to stop the fearful scenes that his imagination insisted on presenting. The night winds screamed a reminder that both his daughters were in grave danger, and he couldn't do anything about it.

To rush out into the storm in an attempt to rescue either of them would be simple suicide. He knew that. Besides, he wasn't even sure where Debbie and Barry were. They'd left the mall hours and hours ago, just before the blizzard hit. Perhaps they'd found shelter in someone's home. Maybe they'd driven into the city, not away from it. At this moment, they might be sitting by a friend's fireplace, sipping hot chocolate and swapping jokes. Or—the man shuddered—they might not be.

"Tyler?" Mr. Hanson heard a gentle voice call from the doorway. "Are you all right?" The lawyer looked up and saw his mother standing just beyond the candle light.

"No, Mom," he whispered, "I'm not all right. I'm terrified. Totally helpless. The storm has captured me. It's holding me prisoner while my little girls are out there beyond my reach. I can't call to them. I can't hold them." He closed his eyes once again. "I feel so very helpless, so afraid."

The woman moved through the shadows and sat down beside her son. "Wendy's safe at Merrilee. It's a strong house and she and Mrs. Dawson will figure out what to do to stay protected."

"But what about Debbie?" Mr. Hanson's voice choked as he spoke. "What's happening to her? The radio already reported that this storm is killing people, good people, folks who weren't prepared. Are my daughter and Barry in trouble, in danger right now, right this very moment?"

The old woman placed her arms around her son. "Tyler, God knows exactly where Debbie is. We've got to believe He's watching over her."

"I wish I could do something, anything!" the lawyer moaned. "It's driving me insane to just sit here and wait, listening to the gale rattle the shutters. I have confidence in Wendy. She's tough, resourceful. I know she and Merrilee are reasonably safe up there in the farmhouse. They'll do the right things. They've got wood and a stove, and John says he took a case of canned beans up there a few days ago. So they'll have something to eat.

"But Debbie is another story. She's so vulnerable, so delicate, like a meadow flower in spring. What does she know about survival, about fighting a storm like this?"

"Don't forget," Grandma Hanson urged, "she's with Wrangler Barry. He knows *everything* about surviving Montana blizzards. He's lived here all his life. That young man's not about to let anything bad happen to Debbie, you can be sure of that." The old woman smiled. "He's a lot like you. He treats our Debbie with such gentleness, and you can tell he cares about her very, very much. So as long as our wrangler friend is anywhere nearby, no harm will come to our little girl."

"It's all my fault," the man said, leaning forward

and pressing his face into his hands. "I shouldn't have come out here. I shouldn't have allowed Debbie to take that job in town. I shouldn't have—"

"Don't be silly," Grandma Hanson interrupted. "I suppose you think you'd all be better off if you shut Wendy and Debbie up in a secure little room and not ever let them out?"

The lawyer lifted his chin. "Only for meals and holidays."

Grandma Hanson chuckled softly. "Well, trust me, Tyler, you'd have some very unhappy children on your hands. Do you think they're sitting wherever they're sitting right now, blaming you for this storm, for the fact that they're caught in it?"

The lawyer didn't answer.

"Children want freedom. But freedom brings risk, sometimes terrible risk. Your father and I have always been very proud of how you've allowed your girls to grow up following their own dreams. You've provided loving support, advice, guidance, discipline, and both Debbie and Wendy are developing into their own wonderful, individual persons. It takes freedom to do that."

The old woman paused. "Remember when you were a child, your father used to tell you the story of Adam and Eve in the Garden of Eden? It was your favorite." Mr. Hanson nodded slowly as his mother continued. "Well, Grandpa used to say that the Creator gave people freedom because He knew that's the only way they'd truly love Him. God knew the risks. He knew sin would roar like a storm across His beautiful new world, placing everyone in terrible danger. He knew innocent people would suffer. That's why He came to earth and lived right here in the middle of the storm with us, so we'd know He knew what we were going through."

The candle flickered in the darkness. "You love Debbie and Wendy so much that you're willing to let them live their lives outside the safe, secure room you wish you could keep them in. It's true that we can't rush out and help them just now, but God can. So, leave them in His hands for one night, Tyler. We'll bring them home after the storm has passed. OK?"

Mr. Hanson's shoulders sagged and tears slipped down his cheeks. "You're right," he said. "That's what I have to do."

He turned and fell to his knees beside the bed. "Oh, God," he prayed, the words tearing from his aching heart, "be with my girls tonight. Keep them safe. Remind them that I love them very much. In Jesus' name, amen."

Grandma Hanson stroked her son's hair in the dim light. She looked through the shadows in the direction of the shuttered window. The wooden slats beyond the glass shook from the force of the gale. She closed her eyes and leaned forward until her cheek rested on top of Tyler's head. "Amen," she whispered.

CHAPTER 5

MORNING

✦ ✦ ✦

Joey stirred. Frigid air hung in the horse barn like an icy curtain, turning the atmosphere into some-thing heavy that pressed down on the small collec-tion of horses and the young boy.

He opened his eyes and blinked a couple times. At first, the teenager wasn't quite sure where he was. He could hear animals nearby, their slow breathing heralding the fact that some were still dozing. What were animals doing in his bedroom?

Joey pulled the covers up until just the tip of his nose was showing. Everything else lay buried under layers of rough cloth.

I think I need some new bedsprings, the lad thought to himself. *These are gettin' kinda hard.* He squirmed. *And what's that awful smell? Maybe it's time for me to wash my socks!*

Joey shook his head as if to clear his thoughts. Now, where was that big, hot dish of mashed potatoes and gravy he'd been enjoying until just a moment ago?

Early snorted and stomped his hoof on the wooden floor. Joey sat up with a start. He'd *never* heard a horse snort in his bedroom before.

"What's goin' on?" he called out into the dimly lit chamber. He looked around. Hey, this wasn't his bedroom in the Station. This was . . . was . . . the barn?

Slowly, ever so slowly, the boy remembered. "Oh, yeah," he moaned, rubbing his chin with his hand. "It really happened. I thought it was a dream."

He flopped back down on the cot. "I'm stuck out here in the barn with five horses and no food." Early snorted again. "No *human* food," the boy corrected. "Horse chow we got. Mashed potatoes and gravy we ain't got."

He sniffed the cold air. "You guys stink!" he called in the direction of the stalls. "Course, it don't help that we're sealed in here like a bunch of Lizzy's peach preserves." He paused. "Maybe you horses think I stink." He lifted an arm to his nose and drew in a deep breath. "Hey, I smell like a horse." The boy smiled. "This should not offend you."

First one leg then another dropped from beneath the covers and landed with a thump on the cold floor. He looked around. Stray shafts of light ap-

91

peared between some of the boards overhead.

"Must be morning," Joey called out to his four-legged companions. He squinted at his wristwatch that hung from a nearby nail. "Hum. Nine o'clock. *Nine o'clock?* Man! I overslept!" He jumped to his feet. "I gotta get up and—" Joey glanced around, then sat back down. "—feed the horses. This is going to be a short commute. I'm already here."

The teenager slowly stretched his legs one at a time, then his arms. He was right in the middle of mid-stretch when he noticed something was different, something other than the fact that it was morning.

"Hey, listen," he called out. Early flipped his ears forward and sniffed the air. "Do you hear it?" Joey queried, walking to the corral door. "Maybe I should say, 'Do you *not* hear it?' The wind. The roaring wind. It's gone. *It's gone!*" The young wrangler danced about the space in front of the horses. "Do you know what that means? Food. *Food!* I'm going to get out of here and eat normal, human food like people are supposed to. No more raw wheat and oats."

The boy ran to the corral door. "Freedom, here I come," he shouted as he unlatched the broad wooden gate. But his excitement came to an abrupt halt when the door would not budge, not even an inch.

"Hey, let me outta here!" he called, even though he knew no one was listening except five curious riding horses.

MORNING

Joey ran across the room and grabbed a stepladder. "I don't believe this," he shouted angrily to himself. The ladder slammed against the small door above the large barn entry. He scurried up the steps and pressed against this secondary opening, which was used to increase the height of the main door when a large object such as a buggy was brought in for repairs. When both doors were utilized, the barn could also accept bulky wagons loaded with hay.

As the smaller portal swung open, Joey's breath caught in his throat. The top of the snow lay just a few feet below his lofty perch. That's why the main door wouldn't budge. It was buried behind a wall of drifted snow. The stuff also covered the pasture, footbridge, creek, orchard, and just about everything else in sight.

Straining to the left, Joey could barely make out the front porch of the Station, beyond where Shadow Creek was supposed to be. The snow had drifted up, almost hiding the first-floor windows. The sight was so unbelievable, so totally incredible, that the boy rubbed his eyes to make sure that what he was looking at really existed.

Slowly, the young wrangler closed the small door and descended the ladder. He went to his cot and sat down heavily on the pile of blankets. "I won't be having breakfast in the Station today," he moaned, glancing toward the stalls. "You'll have to share a few more meals with me. Hope you don't mind."

93

Early and the other horses snorted as if in response.

* * * * *

Wendy scratched her head thoughtfully. She and Merrilee had spent a not-very-comfortable night lying by the woodstove, burning anything that was flammable in the house. The armload of logs the young girl had brought in from the shed just as the storm hit had long ago disappeared up the chimney in the form of smoke and ash, leaving its gift of life-saving heat behind.

During the eternal hours of the night, unused wall paper, burnable building materials, a small pile of yellowing newspapers found in an upstairs closet, one old chair Wendy and Mrs. Dawson had reluctantly decided was of more use to them as heat than a place to sit, a couple of packing boxes used to deliver a load of bathroom tiles and paint supplies, and even the paper labels from the baked-bean cans, including the box they came in, these all had been sacrificed in the stove. The only thing left was the furniture.

"We're not flaming any more of the house stuff," Wendy announced wearily. "You guys gotta have something to sit down on when you move up here."

Merrilee smiled and rubbed her hands together, trying to absorb the last of the heat that radiated from the stove. "What else is there?"

"Wood," Wendy said firmly. "We've got a whole

shed filled with wood right out there." She pointed at the snowed-covered windows. "Let's just go get some."

"We can't walk through that much snow," the woman sighed. "It's over our heads."

"Then we'll tunnel through it," Wendy urged.

"What if it caves in and buries us alive?"

The girl nodded reluctantly. "Good point." She sat silently for a moment, pondering the situation. The house was still a little warm, but in a few hours the temperature inside would drop below freezing. They'd be in danger. Real danger.

Yes. They had to have that wood. It was the only solution left to the problem.

Wendy's eyes suddenly brightened. Merrilee saw a grin begin to twitch at the corners of the young girl's mouth, then a smile that spread from ear to ear.

"Wendy Hanson, what on earth are you mulling around in that brain of yours?" the woman asked hesitantly. "If those stories I've heard about you are true, I don't think I'm going to like what you have up your sleeve."

The girl tilted her head. "What stories?"

"Well, there was this thing about a curse in the attic, a rock with glowing eyes—"

"Oh, those," the girl shrugged. "Ancient history."

"Yeah, right," Merrilee chuckled. "You're not thinking of calling up some ancient spirit to get that wood for us, are you?"

Wendy laughed out loud. "Don't you know there

aren't any spirits *or* curses? That's just a bunch of old-time Indian mumbo-jumbo." She paused. "Besides, we don't need any voodoo, 'cause I've got a plan."

"A plan?"

"Yup. In no time we'll be sitting here as warm as a wooly worm in a tree trunk."

The woman's eyes narrowed. "And just how do you expect to get wood out of a shed that's buried up to its eaves in a drift?"

Wendy leaned forward. "Well, you see all that snow out there?"

"I did notice a few flakes."

The girl grinned. "We can't go *through* it."

"Nope."

"Can't go *under* it."

"Nope."

"Then," Wendy said, rising to her feet. "We'll go *over* it."

"Over it?"

"Yup. Just like Tarzan."

* * * * *

Debbie sat in the stillness of the truck bed, watching her companion sleep. It was dark. Only a faint glow of reflected daylight reached the buried vehicle through the air passage. That's how the girl realized night had finally ended and a new day had begun.

By placing her ear right next to the tube, she could hear that the winds had gone, too. There was no way she could be sure if it had stopped snowing. She could only hope the storm had spent its fury and moved on to the southeast.

The night had been long. Barry's condition had worsened rapidly. He complained of terrible pains in his chest and had coughed up blood several times. After one such agonizing spell, he'd provided his own diagnosis.

"My broken ribs must have punctured something inside me," he'd gasped, his face pale in the harsh radiance of the flashlight. "Maybe even a lung."

At first, Debbie had been terrified, unable to speak. The seriousness of their situation had pressed down on her shoulders like an unbearable weight. But then the terror had passed, leaving behind a stubborn resolve to survive.

She'd made the wrangler as comfortable as possible, covering him gently with as many blankets as she could find. She figured if his ribs were causing the damage, he must not move. This would only make things worse. She also knew that if they were going to be rescued at all, she'd have to be the one to figure out a way to make it happen.

After Barry had fallen into a restless sleep, she busied herself securing the truck. Things useless to them were stored in the passenger side of the big cab. The several bags of groceries Barry had picked up for Grandma Hanson were carefully sorted and placed nearby, ready to provide energy for the hours and perhaps days ahead.

Although she was cold, Debbie discovered that Barry had been right—snow acts as a very effective insulator against freezing winds. She'd even limited the flow of air down the pipe by securing a flap of duct tape over the end of the tube. When it began to get too cold, she'd lessen the flow. If things got a little stuffy, she opened it back up again.

Now, as she sat in the stillness, watching Barry sleep, her mind was busy with thoughts of rescue. She spoke in the cold air even though she knew her companion didn't hear.

"OK. This is the situation. We're buried under about 12 feet of drifted snow. We've got food and protection to last us for a couple days, longer if necessary. Barry's hurt badly and must not move an inch. I can melt small amounts of snow for drinking water by breathing on it. We've got a flashlight with fresh batteries, and all the PVC pipe we'd need to transport water from here to New Mexico."

The girl adjusted her position on the small pile of feed sacks. "What I've got to do is figure out a way of telling people up there that we're down here." Debbie leaned her head against the wall of the truck bed. "But they're not going to know where to look, are they? I'm sure the phone lines are down and the power is off all over this area, so I better not get my hopes for a quick rescue up too high."

She glanced down at her injured friend. She could

just make out the features of his face outlined by the dim light radiating from the air pipe. "I wanted to spend some time with you," she said, "but this wasn't exactly what I had in mind."

Debbie saw the young man's face grimace as the pain in his chest prodded his sleep like a bully poking a classmate with a stick.

"Please be OK, Barry," she breathed. "I don't know what to do to help you. You need to be OK."

The wrangler coughed quietly and stirred. Debbie adjusted the blankets about his shoulders and whispered, "Lie still, cowboy. You've got to stay motionless until help gets here." The horseman's breathing relaxed as he drifted into deeper slumber. "That's right," the girl nodded. "Sleep. Dream of horses and sunny pastures." She paused, then bent low until her lips were close to his ear. "And if you want to, you could even dream of me. I wouldn't mind."

Debbie's voice choked in the darkness. "Just don't die," she said, a tear slipping down her flushed cheek. "Please, Barry, please don't die."

* * * * *

"Base to Joey. Base to Joey." Grandpa Hanson stood out on the freshly shoveled porch that fronted his son's office. From his second-story perch he could make out the upper half of the horse barn.

"Joey to base." The walkie-talkie crackled to life. "Hi, Grandpa Hanson. You guys still kickin' over there?"

99

"I was just going to ask you the same question. Over."

He heard his young ranch hand chuckle. "Oh, me and the horses are doing just fine. We've started a club. Wanna join?"

"Not right now," Grandpa Hanson laughed. "Looks like you might be able to see out of the upper door if you wanted to. Over."

"Yeah. I already did. Big deal. Just a bunch of snow piled everywhere. Here, I'll show you."

The old man stood waiting, surveying the ocean of white that spread across his valley to the towering mountains beyond. The view was impressive and would have been all the more so if everyone were safe and sound in the Station.

He looked to the east, in the direction of Squaw Rock. He knew that up there, in one of the folds in the mountains, Wendy and Merrilee were being held captive by the incredible drifts of snow.

"Hey, Grandpa Hanson. Do you see me?" The rancher heard a voice calling from a distance. He laughed when he saw Joey hanging out of the upper doorway of the barn. He clicked off his walkie-talkie and cupped his hands to his mouth. "Hi, Joey. You look like you survived well enough. Are the horses taking good care of you?"

"Oh, we're regular pals, except somebody over here stinks to high heaven and it ain't me, no matter what the horses may say."

The old man chuckled. "You'd better clean out the stalls."

He saw Joey pause, then look around. "Just where am I supposed to put the manure?"

"Good question," Grandpa Hanson called back, his voice echoing across the distance "Just carry it up there and throw it out across the top of the snow. Frozen horse pies are a whole lot less smelly than fresh ones."

"You're right," the teenager shouted back. "Excuse me while I get to work." With a wave Joey disappeared into the barn. In a few moments, Grandpa Hanson saw a shovelful of manure fly out of the opening and bury itself in the clean white snow. This was soon followed by another. Then another.

Samantha stumbled out onto the porch and joined the old man at the railing. She stood watching the strange goings on at the distant barn.

"What's Joey doing?" she asked, her words muffled by the scarf she wore tightly wrapped around her face.

"He's cleaning out the stalls," Grandpa Hanson said.

Another load of manure flew through the open doorway and arched out across the snow. "There goes Pookie's poop," the little girl announced. "I can tell."

The old man laughed out loud. "You get back into the house," he ordered with a grin. "It's too cold out here for little girls with lots of curls."

Samantha nodded. "OK. Tell Joey I'll come and visit him just as soon as I get my snow boat finished."

"You're building a snow boat?"

"Yup. Me and Pueblo will just sail out there and rescue Joey and the horses and bring them back here to the Station."

Grandpa Hanson chuckled. "Well, I think I may have a better idea. Come on, I'll show you."

The little girl followed her friend back into the big Station and up the stairs that led to the attic. The old man looked around, lifting a box here and moving a piece of dusty furniture there.

"What are we looking for?" Samantha asked, peering behind a pile of burlap bags.

"These," Grandpa Hanson announced triumphantly as he bent and picked up what looked like a pair of tennis rackets.

"What're those?" the little girl gasped, fingering the tightly strung, wooden frames. "Are you going to play a game with Joey?"

"Nope," the old man said. "Mr. Hanson's gonna rescue him."

"How?"

The rancher searched and found another pair of the strange looking devices. "He's gonna just walk over to the barn and bring him back. You wanna watch?"

"You bet!" Samantha cried.

"Well then, let's get going," the old man encouraged.

102

"Let's get goin'," his companion repeated as they clamored back down the attic stairs and made their way to the office porch.

The young lawyer was waiting by the railing, dressed in layers of warm sweaters and coats. "You sure this is going to work?" he asked his father as the two approached.

"Got any other ideas?" the old man chuckled.

"Fresh out," Mr. Hanson admitted. He turned toward the barn just in time to see something fly through the upper door and disappear into the snow.

"What was that?" the man gasped.

"Pookie poop," Samantha explained.

Mr. Hanson blinked. "Pookie what?"

The old man giggled. "Oh, yeah, you might want to tell Joey you're coming before you get there. Wouldn't want you to get a face full of Pookie poop if you appear at the opening unannounced."

Samantha watched as Mr. Hanson tied those strange looking objects from the attic onto his feet. The other pair he hung over his shoulder. Then slowly, carefully, Grandpa Hanson helped his son ease over the railing and lower himself with a rope to the surface of the snow below.

"Now, keep your feet far apart so you won't trip," the older man called as the rescuer with the funny shoes adjusted his position on the snow. "The drifts have had time to settle so you shouldn't experience too many problems. Just don't fall over. You might not be able to get up again 'til spring."

Mr. Hanson nodded. "That's good to know." He let go of the rope and took a few uncertain steps forward.

"That's it," Grandpa Hanson called. "You're doin' fine. Just pretend the snow is rock solid. Don't think of it as something that could bury you alive."

"Enough with the encouragement. Just don't lose sight of me in case you have to come dig me out."

"Can't," the old man stated. "You've got both pairs of snowshoes."

The lawyer paused, then continued. "Remind me to buy a few more of these gizmos at the hardware store next time we're in Bozeman."

"Already on the shopping list," his father responded.

Ever so carefully, Mr. Hanson made his way toward the distant corral. He saw that the surface of the snow dipped slightly and took that to be Shadow Creek. As he stood catching his breath, he could hear the muffled sound of water running somewhere far below.

Joey scooped the last of the manure from the stalls and sent it hurling through the open door above the main corral entrance. He was about to climb the ladder and secure the portal when he heard his name being called.

"Hey, Joey. Stop throwing stuff out the door."

The teenager ran to the walkie-talkie and pressed the transmit button. "Is that you, Mr. H? How ya doin'?"

The lawyer's face appeared at the opening over-head. "You want to get back to the Station, or do you like it out here with the horses?"

Joey sighed. "Man, I wanna be with you guys like nothin' else, but I'm stuck. No way out. Over."

Mr. Hanson realized that Joey thought his voice was coming from the walkie-talkie. He covered his mouth to suppress a giggle. "Tell you what I'll do," the lawyer called, trying to make his words sound electronically reproduced. "You promise to make my bed for a month and polish my boots every Friday afternoon and I'll come out and rescue you right now. Over."

Joey brightened. "Sure!" he gasped. "You get me back to the Station and I'll do anything. But how you gonna do it? Snow's too deep. Over."

A loud clattering made the young wrangler jump sideways, just as something landed at his feet. He looked down to discover a pair of snowshoes in the straw. Glancing up, he saw Mr. Hanson's smiling face grinning down at him from the opening above the main door.

"Mr. H!" Joey cried out excitedly. "You've come to save me. Now I can eat. Now I can be warm!" He paused. "Wait a minute. You tricked me. I thought you were in the Station."

"Details, details," the lawyer called down. "Just slip those do-dads on your big feet and we'll waltz right back to the house."

Joey shook his head and retrieved the snowshoes. "Man, you got me good. But I don't care." He climbed the ladder and sat on the ledge of the opening. He quickly fastened the devices to his boots and swung his feet out onto the surface of the snow. "I forgot Grandpa Hanson had these. Showed 'em to me last winter. Never needed 'em 'til now."

As the two made their way along the expanse of white, Joey chuckled. "Now I've got to make your bed for a week."

"Month."

"And shine your dirty ol' shoes. Man, you tricked me good. But it's OK. I didn't think I'd *ever* get rescued."

"Now we've got to concentrate on the rest of the family," his companion sighed as they moved along. "Soon as the road crews restore power and phone service, we've got to find Debbie and Barry and get up to Merrilee."

Joey reached over carefully and tapped his friend on the shoulder. Mr. Hanson turned. "We'll find 'em," Joey smiled. "We'll get everyone home safe and sound. You'll see."

The man nodded and continued walking carefully in the direction of the big Station.

* * * * *

"This is not going to work." Mrs. Dawson stood leaning out of the upstairs window of the small homestead, her arms tightly wrapped around Wendy's legs.

The girl studied the length of rope that stretched

between her hands and the tree limb about 20 feet above and away from the house. "Of course it's going to work. Haven't you ever seen a Tarzan movie? He zooms from tree to tree as easy as you please. I just have to swing over to the shed. Piece of cake."

"Tarzan is Hollywood. This is Montana. There's a big difference, you know."

Wendy ignored her companion's complaints. "You just make sure you don't let go of the second rope I've tied to the main rope. I'll tie the logs to the main rope, and with that second rope you can pull them here to the window. And you'll be able to pull me back when we've gotten all the wood out of the shed. I think it's a terrific plan. I got this rope over that limb up there, didn't I?"

Merrilee shivered in the icy air. "I don't like this. I think we should just burn the furniture. You might get hurt or something."

"Don't worry. I've got it all figured out. My swing should carry me right over the shed. I'll just land gently on the roof, knock a whole in the boards with this hammer, ease down through the opening, and start bringing those big, beautiful logs up for you to haul in." She tightened her grip on the rope. "Now, let go."

The woman reluctantly loosened her hold on Wendy's legs. With a war whoop that would make Red Stone the Indian proud, the girl dropped out into space. Merrilee watched as she sailed away from the farmhouse, out across the snow-buried yard. Her feet skimmed the drifts as she picked up speed.

Wendy felt her weight increase as she raced across the snow. She saw the shed rush toward her, then begin to drop as she swung up, up, up. Her hands gripped the rough cord until her knuckles turned white.

Maybe this wasn't such a good idea after all, she thought to herself as she watched tree branches whip past.

Reaching the end of her swing, she felt her body go weightless for a second, then begin to drop again. She glanced down and found she was right above the snow-covered shed. She knew that if she didn't time herself just right she wouldn't land on the structure at all but would be carried past it. There was only one thing to do. Let go.

Merrilee saw the girl release her grip on the line and fall straight down. She screamed as Wendy's body slammed into the roof and disappeared through splintering boards and swirls of snow. A muffled crash reverberated from somewhere inside the structure. Then everything was still.

"Wendy! Wendy!" the woman cried, fear straining her words. Oh, why had she allowed such a hairbrained idea in the first place? Now Wendy was badly hurt and she couldn't even go out to help her.

A hand, then an arm, then a head appeared through the large, gaping hole in the shed's roof. "Wow. What a ride!" she heard Wendy call out excitedly. "Landing was a little less graceful than I'd planned, but here I am." The young girl spread her arms apart, a smile lighting her flushed face. "Ta-da!" she trumpeted.

Merrilee sat down on the window ledge, trying to still her racing heart. "You scared me to death," she called. "I thought you were dead for sure."

"All in a day's work," the girl responded gleefully. "Hooray for Hollywood!"

The woman laughed with relief as Wendy leaned back and beat her chest with her fists. "Ahh-ee-aaahh-eee-ahhh." The call of Tarzan echoed through the snow-covered pines and cottonwoods of Gallatin National Forest.

CHAPTER 6

THE SUBSTITUTE

❂ ❂ ❂

The day stretched tiringly into the afternoon hours. Every 15 minutes or so, Mr. Hanson would get up from his spot by the fireplace and walk to the hall phone. He'd pick up the receiver and place it against his ear. Then the lawyer would quietly return the handset to its cradle and walk back into the warm den.

Joey and the others would shake their heads sadly. The man's quick return meant the phone lines were still dead. Communication with the outside world was still impossible.

No one wanted to talk about Wendy, Merrilee, and Debbie, yet the missing members, especially Debbie, were on everyone's mind. It was almost cruel to be able to look out of the upstairs windows and see the mountains, knowing that Wendy and Merrilee were up there—so close, yet so far.

And what about Debbie and Barry? Were they all right? Were they hurt? The agony of waiting began to tell on those gathered by the flickering flames.

"I've got to do something!" Mr. Hanson slammed his fist onto the arm of his chair. "I'll go crazy if I don't."

Grandpa Hanson sighed a frustrated sigh. "There's nothing you can do. All the roads are—"

"I know that!" his son interrupted with a voice charged with anger. "You don't have to remind me. But I can't just sit here while my daughters are in danger." He jumped to his feet. "I'm going out. I can try for Merrilee with the snowshoes. They got me to the barn."

"Tyler, No!" the old man commanded. "Joey was just across the creek. John's homestead is five miles away. And what if there's an avalanche, or darkness comes before you get there? And what if it starts to snow again?"

"DON'T TELL ME WHY I CAN'T DO THIS. TELL ME WHY I CAN!" The man's face was lined with tension.

Grandpa Hanson lifted his hands. "There *is* no *can*, Tyler," he said gently. "And what good are you to anyone if you freeze to death out there? Road crews out of Bozeman are working around the clock. The power and phone people are right behind them, doing their best to restore service to all the hard-hit areas. Don't forget that our very own neighbor, Ned, works for the county. He was away from home when the storm struck. He'll be anxious to get back to his wife, and trust me, he'll bring the big highway snow-blowers with him."

He paused. "Besides, for all we know, Debbie and Barry may be already found. So just sit down and wait with the rest of us."

The lawyer paused at the door and bowed his head. After a long moment he spoke. "It hurts, Dad. It hurts my heart to feel so helpless."

Grandpa Hanson stood and walked over to his son. Placing a hand on his shoulder he said quietly, "All we can do is pray, Tyler. That's the only action available to us right now."

The younger man turned and gazed into his father's eyes. "But I don't feel like praying, Dad."

The old man nodded. "That doesn't mean God won't hear. He knows our hearts are hurting. He understands what it's like to be afraid and feel far from the source of strength that we need. Remember what Christ said on the cross? In His darkest hour, Jesus cried out, 'Father. Why have You forsaken me?'

"God knows what you're feeling, Tyler. He knows . . . and hears."

Mr. Hanson nodded slowly, then walked out into the hallway. Pausing by the phone he lifted the receiver, then placed it back on its cradle and climbed the cold steps leading to the second floor.

Those gathered in the den heard him enter Debbie's room and quietly close the door.

* * * * *

The last log swung from the top of the shed, across the snow-blanketed farmyard, and to the upstairs window. Merrilee pulled it into the bedroom and loosened the knot, letting the chunk of wood thump to the floor.

The room was littered with carefully cut lengths of firewood, enough to see the hard-working, snow-bound pair through days of captivity in their little mountain home.

"That's it," Wendy called, her arms aching from the hours of lifting, tying, swinging, and hauling. "That'll keep us toasty warm for a long time. And look what else I found." She held up a couple of tin cups and an old, bent spoon she'd discovered on a shelf in the shed. "Not exactly uptown, but at least we can drink water out of something other than a cooking pot."

"Only one spoon?" Merrilee responded from the window. "Guess we'll have to share. At least we can have hot beans for supper and give our fingers a rest."

Wendy chuckled. "Don't say the word *beans*. Let's pretend that for tonight we're going to have macaroni and cheese or something." The big rope swung in her direction and Wendy caught it as it passed by. "And we're not going to be drinking water. It'll be hot chocolate or some of Grandma Hanson's steamy herb tea with honey in it."

The girl tied the rope around her waist then took a firm hold on the rough line. "Now you're going to have to get me swinging really high so I can make it up there. Just tug on the secondary rope each time I'm headin' in your direction."

"OK," Merrilee agreed. "But be careful."

Wendy stepped back a few feet from the edge of the shed, then ran forward, launching herself out over the snow.

The woman pulled hard, then allowed her companion to swing away from her.

Back and forth, higher and higher the girl oscillated, like a human pendulum, traveling further and further with each pass. Soon, she could just about reach the window ledge with her toes. Two more arching swings and she dove through the opening. Merrilee grabbed her around the waist.

For a moment, they thought they'd both be pulled back out of the window as Wendy began her return trip, but the woman's strength prevailed. The girl quickly unfastened the rope and they dropped to the floor, tired, happy, victorious.

"See, I told you it would work," the grinning youngster teased. "I may not be the smartest, most talented, or prettiest girl in the world, but I can get wood out of an old shed any day."

Merrilee chuckled. "Well, I think you're smart, talented, and pretty, all rolled into one. You saw a problem, worked out a plan, and got busy. That's how it's done."

Wendy stumbled to her feet and surveyed the random piles of logs scattered about the room. "Not a bad haul, even if I say so myself."

The woman nodded. "But they're not going to do us any good up here. Let's get a couple loads downstairs and make that stove earn its keep. I can feel the temperature dropping. Sun's going down. We'll need all the heat we can get tonight."

The two gathered armloads of the dry logs and clamored down the stairs. "I'm hungry," Wendy moaned. "What's for supper?"

"Bea—" Merrilee stopped mid-word. "Make that macaroni and cheese, with hot chocolate and wheat bread."

"Good choice," the girl giggled. "Fresh strawberry pie would be nice too."

"Oh, no," Merrilee called. "Gotta save that for breakfast."

* * * * *

Night slipped in from the east, covering the frozen land with silvery shadows. Day disappeared without a sound, without a trace; it left nothing in its wake but silent drifts of snow and fearful hearts.

Debbie watched the dim light at the base of the air passage slowly fade. In her silent world, the only sounds were her breathing, and the occasional moan from her fitfully sleeping companion.

She gently stroked the wrangler's hair with her fingers. *Funny how the human body insists on sleeping when it's trying to heal,* Debbie thought to herself. She adjusted the blankets covering the young man's shoulders. *Maybe this is what it's like to die. You just hurt some, then go to sleep. Isn't that what the preacher kept saying last Sabbath at church—death is like sleep? You close your eyes and then you see Jesus coming?*

Dying wouldn't be so bad. Who wants to suffer through life, anyway? Who wants to see friends hurt, watch people die, read about nations murdering nations. Life's hard on everybody. Dying seems like such a good idea.

Debbie shook her head. "What am I thinking?" she said aloud. "I don't want to die. I want to live. I want to be with Dad and Wendy. I want to design pretty dresses and fix up window displays in department stores."

The girl stared into the darkness. "And," her voice softened, "I want to fall in love and get married and have children—two children—a boy and girl. I want to do something important for other people, something that will make them happy, something that will make the world better for everyone."

She sighed. "Most of all, I want to get Barry and me out of this truck. He needs a doctor. He needs to get to the hospital where they can fix his ribs and find out what's wrong inside."

Debbie sat silent for a long moment. "I want to

know what it's like to have someone, a guy, love me and think I'm the most wonderful person in the whole world."

"You sure don't want much," a weak voice spoke in the darkness.

Debbie gasped. "Barry? You awake?"

The wrangler chuckled painfully. "How can anyone sleep with all this gabbing going on?"

Debbie reddened. "Oh, no. How long have you been awake?"

"Long enough to know that the world better be prepared when we get out of here. You're a woman on a mission."

The girl buried her face in her hands. "You weren't supposed to hear all that. I was just thinking out loud. Oh, I'm so embarrassed."

"Hey." The girl felt a hand touch her arm. "It's OK. I like what you said. Those were good things, important things. You sounded like Judy."

"Judy?" the word was spoken with not a lot of enthusiasm. "She your girlfriend or something?"

"Nah. Just a classmate, although we were supposed to go to the game this Sunday. Don't think we'll make it."

There was a long pause, then Debbie spoke in the darkness. "What's she like?"

"Oh, I don't know, just a girl. She thinks she's going to revolutionize modern medicine with herbs. Probably will. There's nothing more powerful than a woman on a mission."

"Is she pretty?"

The wrangler coughed quietly. Debbie could feel his hand tighten around her arm as the pains in his chest reminded the horseman of his injuries. "She's OK. Not as pretty as you."

"Oh, I'm not all that great."

The girl heard her companion chuckle. "Debbie Hanson, you're about the prettiest thing I've ever seen—especially when you do your hair up, like when I took you to that job interview at the mall. You looked just like a fashion model or something."

The girl reached up and touched a length of long, dark hair cascading past her face. "You really think so? I mean, do you really think I'm pretty?"

"Whadda I gotta do, sign something? Yes. You're beautiful. Any guy would be proud to have you as his girlfriend."

Debbie let her hand drop back to her lap. "Any guy, huh? I'll try to remember that."

Barry shifted his position, groaning as the pain in his chest racked his prone body. "That includes me," the voice in the darkness said softly. "But I know I'm way out of your league."

Debbie blinked. "What? What did you say?"

Barry's hand tightened again as a groan escaped his lips. "Man, I hurt bad, Debbie," he said. "I'm sorry you have to take care of me like this."

"I don't mind," the girl responded breathlessly. "I'll take care of you until we can get you to a hospital. I promise."

The man's breathing steadied. "Thanks, Debbie. You're the best. You're the very best."

Weariness and pain overcame the horseman and he slipped into an uneasy slumber. Debbie sat in the darkness, stroking his head with gentle fingers. "I was wrong," she whispered, her words unheard by her injured companion. "What I really want the most . . . is you."

* * * * *

R-r-ring. The sound of a telephone echoed through the midnight halls of the Station. Mr. Hanson jerked, wide awake, listening. Had he heard something?

R-r-ring. He leaped to his feet, hands trembling. "THE PHONE! It's working again!" he cried out, trying to make his way past the stirring bodies scattered across the den rug like leaves in a field.

R-r-ring. Stumbling out into the lobby, the lawyer fumbled for the phone in the murky darkness. "Debbie? DEBBIE?" he shouted into the receiver.

Grandpa Hanson appeared at the doorway, his form silhouetted against the dim glow radiating from the fireplace.

"Yes. This is Tyler Hanson." The man listened intently as he shivered in the cold. "Yes. Her name is Debbie. She's with Barry Gordon, a student at the University. They left the mall around 4:00 or 5:00 yesterday, just before the storm hit. No, I'm not sure which way they were heading, but I assume they were trying for the ranch. Now that the phones are working, she may call in."

Mr. Hanson stood listening to the voice in the receiver. "Yes, please," he said, his words filled with newfound excitement. "At first light. I understand. And we'll call if they make contact with us before then."

Grandpa Hanson could hear a distant, electronic voice buzzing from the handset at his son's ear. "Oh, thank you," the young lawyer called out. "Let me know if anything . . . if you find anything. Just call immediately, OK? I'll be waiting. Goodbye."

The man hung up the phone and turned to face his father. "That was the police in Bozeman. They talked to the security guard at the mall and he told them about Debbie and Barry heading out just before the storm. The officer said that the big snowblowers are clearing Highway 191 as we speak and that they'll send one this way at first light."

The old man wrapped his arms around his son and held him close. "We'll find them tomorrow, Tyler. I promise. They'll be OK."

Mr. Hanson let out a long, heartrending cry. The weight of fear had finally overcome him, causing his knees to buckle. Together, father and son dropped to the floor and sat in each other's embrace for a long moment. "Oh, dear God," the young lawyer sobbed, "don't leave her. Don't let her go. Please. Just one more night. Please, God."

Grandpa Hanson tightened his grip on the weeping man as they sat shadowed by the yellow glow from the hearth. One by one, the other Station inhabitants made their way into the cold lobby and added their arms of support until the crying man found himself completely surrounded by people who cared for him.

Far away, through the hours of darkness, powerful snowblowers driven by dedicated highway workers lumbered along, sending fountains of snow rising into the frigid air. Inch by inch, mile by mile, they moved through the half-moon shadows, closing the distance between them and the little ranch in the valley.

* * * * *

"Merrilee? Are you awake?" The question came softly, like the rustle of dry leaves across the frozen face of the forest.

"Is something wrong?" the woman said, sitting up quickly. "Is the fire going out?"

The living room was warm and cozy, the hard-won logs doing their duty in the stove's crackling, ember-red firebox.

"No. I'm OK. I just wanted to ask you something."

Merrilee lay back down against the rug, her head resting on a rolled-up window curtain. "I was dreaming," she said. "You, me, and John were in Florida, on the beach, enjoying a very hot sun." She chuckled. "Strange. You were swinging from the yardarm of some pirate ship out beyond the breakers. I told you

121

to be careful, but you just insisted you had to get the logs."

Wendy giggled. "Now where did such a silly dream come from?"

"I wonder," the woman grinned.

The two were silent for a moment. "I wanted to ask you something," the girl said softly.

"Well, now that I'm not on a beach in Florida getting a suntan, ask away."

Wendy rose up on one elbow. "When you were my age, did you miss your real mother? You know. When she died in the car crash?"

A stray gust of wind sprinkled snow against the window, then blew past. Wendy heard her companion sigh deeply. "I thought my world had ended," the woman began. "I was at school when the police car pulled into the parking lot. I watched the man get out and slowly close the door. He seemed sad, nervous, as if he didn't want to do what he'd been assigned.

"He came in and talked to my teacher and they kept looking over at me. Then Mrs. Waterman asked me to follow her out into the hallway.

"I remember I had a library book in my hand— one about birds. It had a big hawk on the cover. She told me that there'd been an accident and that my mom and dad wouldn't be coming to get me after school. She said they'd both been killed. To this day, I can't look at a hawk flying overhead without thinking about how much I miss my parents."

Wendy was silent for several minutes. When she

spoke, her words sounded very, very tired. "Sometimes I wish my mother had died. Then I'd know why I couldn't see her anymore. But then I'm glad she's alive because I love her." She turned to face Merrilee. "Is it awful for me to say that I wish my mother had died?"

The woman stared at the firelight dancing across the ceiling. "I don't think so," she said. "Sometimes death is easier to take, easier to understand, than divorce. I've known many children whose parents have split up. It's like they see their security, their happy home, crumble right before their eyes. But then, unlike death, they see someone they love, someone they depend on, simply move out, walk away, start a new life somewhere else." Merrilee looked into the eyes of her young friend. "Death and divorce are very much alike. But when two people stop loving each other, there's no funeral, no memorial service, because both are still alive, still a part of life. In many, many ways, divorce is the harder to accept."

Wendy lay back on her makeshift pillow. "My mom used to take me shopping. We'd go to bunches of stores and she'd buy me lots of dresses and white gloves and shiny shoes. I'd try everything on and she'd get all gushy and stuff about how *won-der-ful* I looked. It made me feel like I was really special, really important."

The woman smiled slightly. "You used to wear

dresses? I mean, real girl-type dresses, with bows and lace?"

"Yup," Wendy said. "But when Mom left, I gave them all to the community welfare store around the corner from our apartment building. They were silly, anyway. I looked like a real jerk in 'em."

Merrilee shook her head. "I'll bet you looked nice."

"Maybe," the girl responded. "But they were sorta like your hawk. They made me remember. That hurt too much."

Wendy slowly got up and walked to the living room window. Through the trees she could see the first hint of dawn touching the distant mountain tops. She stood there, not knowing what to say or even why she'd shared her deepest, most painful thoughts with a woman who'd had troubles of her own when she was young.

"We're a lot alike, you and me," Merrilee called softly. "We both have painful pasts. We both have scars on our hearts from things that happened— things we had no control over."

Wendy studied the dark outlines of the mountains against the soft glow of the sky. "Does the pain ever go away?" she asked.

"No, not really. You just have to learn to live with it."

"How?"

Merrilee joined her friend at the window. "It's kind of a decision. You decide that one part of your life, one important part in this case, is past, gone, finished. But life must go on. You can't relive the years that have vanished. So you cry your last tear, pick up the pieces of your broken heart, and march on, asking the Lord to help you heal. He's good at that. Had plenty of practice."

Merrilee heard her companion sob softly. "Will you help me?" Wendy asked. "Will you show me how?"

"Of course," the woman responded, her eyes glistening.

The young girl turned and gazed up at Merrilee. "There're so many questions I want to ask. So many things I wonder about. My dad doesn't know what to say when we talk about certain stuff. Debbie's always too busy with her dresses and drawings, and I'm too embarrassed to ask Grandpa or Grandma about the things I want to know. Can I come visit you and we can talk about stuff and you can tell me why I feel certain ways and what's going to happen to me as I get older? Then I won't feel so scared all the time. Then I might not miss my mother so much."

Merrilee encircled Wendy with warm, loving arms. "Tell you what, partner. If you'd like, I can be your substitute mother for as long as you want me to. John and I have never been able to have children of our own, even though we've tried for years and years. So you can sorta be my substitute daughter, too. Looks like it might be a good deal for both of us. How's it sound to you?"

Wendy was silent for a long moment. Merrilee felt the girl relax in her arms, then she saw a smile spread across the young, tearstained face.

"You're not going to make me wear dresses or anything, are you?"

The woman shrugged. "Well, maybe once in a while, just to remind me that you're a girl."

"No pink ones," the youngster giggled. "And no bows. I hate bows."

"Deal," Merrilee announced, thrusting out her hand. "No pink and no bows."

Wendy reached out as if to shake her companion's hand, then paused. She looked up into the gentle eyes gazing down at her. "Once I thought that the treasure of the Merrilee might be a pile of gold. But now I know better. It's love, isn't it? Mrs. Grant knew it. Now we do, too. Isn't that right?"

"That's exactly right." The woman smiled. "In this world, there's nothing more valuable than old-fashioned love."

Beyond the ice-rimmed window panes, a new day was dawning. For Wendy Hanson, the storm had finally passed.

CHAPTER 7

RESCUE

◎ ◎ ◎

A sharp *snap* resonated from the embers that lay in small, shimmering piles in the soot-darkened fireplace. The den was silent except for the soft breathing of prone figures snuggled inside fluffy sleeping bags and under blankets.

Grandma Hanson opened an eye, unsure, at first, of where the sound had come from. Slowly she rose on one elbow and looked around the dimly lit den. The room had no color, only silver-gray, the same hue as the eastern sky beyond the windows.

A shadowy form by the door caught her eye. Someone was sitting up in a chair, fully dressed, with hat, earmuffs, gloves, and boots in place. A pair of snowshoes leaned against the nearby wall.

The old woman smiled a hopeful smile. Today her

precious son would be reunited with his daughters, her granddaughters. She knew it. The lady wasn't sure why, but she just knew today would bring an end to the fear and hopelessness that filled Tyler's heart, filled her heart.

The man in the chair nodded, his sleep fitful. Dawn would not catch him unprepared. He'd dressed for the challenge hours ago, after the phone call from the Bozeman police.

"Tyler?" Grandma Hanson called quietly.

She saw her son jump to his feet. "I'm ready. Let's go!" The man looked about the room, then over at his mother. "Oh," he said, "I thought maybe the blowers had come."

"I'm sorry," the woman apologized. "I didn't mean to startle you. I just wanted to suggest that you get some warm food in your stomach before you head out. Joey and Mr. Dawson, too. You'll all need strength for the search."

"Food?" A muffled voice called from deep inside a sleeping bag by the window. "Did someone say food?"

Joey's nose and eyes appeared from under the pile of cloth. "I ain't never gonna refuse chow again in my whole life."

Mr. Hanson chuckled. "I might be too nervous to eat anything, but it sounds like a good idea. I'll get John up, just as soon as I figure out which pile is him."

"Don't bother," came a reply from the direction of

the fireplace. With a quick move, the top of a sleeping bag flipped back, revealing a man completely dressed, with boots and gloves. "And let's pack a supply of eatables for our two castaways at Merrilee. I'm sure they're kinda tired of baked beans by now."

One by one, the other members of the survival slumber party awoke and began readying themselves for the hours ahead. Voices were guardedly cheerful. For the first time in two days, their words carried a hint of genuine hope. Today, the lost would be found. Today, heart-numbing questions would be answered. Today, Wendy, Merrilee, Debbie, and Barry would be rescued from the monster's grip.

Busy bodies moved through the cold, gray-lit halls and rooms of the big Station. Faces were washed in the kitchen sink, using water heated on the gas cooking stove.

Steaming bowls of vegetable stew, along with thick, soft-crusted slices of wheat bread, disappeared down eager throats. Each Station inhabitant wanted to be fully prepared for what the day might bring.

Even as they ate, their ears were tuned to catch the first sounds of the approaching blowers. Tension and expectation mounted as the seconds ticked by.

* * * * *

"Barry?" Debbie leaned close to her friend and spoke softly in his ear. "Barry, wake up."

"What? What is it?"

"I hear something."

The injured man blinked his eyes open and coughed quietly, flinching at the pains in his chest. "I don't hear anything."

"No. Listen. It's coming down the tube." Debbie scrambled to the broken window that separated the cab from the truck's bed. She placed her ear next to the opening of the plastic air pipe and lifted a finger. "There. Do you hear it? Sounds like a machine or something."

Barry tilted his head slightly. Yes. There was a new noise echoing down the airway, one they hadn't heard before. It sounded like a rumbling, a churning, like a train going by. But there were no tracks in this area. What would a train be doing—

"Wait." The wrangler grimaced at the movement his word brought to his chest. "It's a truck. A big truck."

"How can it be?" Debbie questioned. "Snow's too deep. There's no way a truck could be driving by."

"It could if it was pushing a snowblower," the young man said, his words strained.

"A snowblower? You mean one of those big highway jobs?"

"Yup. We're about to get rescued, Miss Fashion Designer."

Debbie let out a loud war whoop and clapped her hands together. "You think so? I mean you really think so?"

"We're off the main highway," Barry said between gritted teeth. "The only reason they'd be out here on this road would be that they're trying to reach Shadow Creek Ranch. They must be looking for us."

"We're saved. WE'RE SAVED!" The girl flattened herself on the pile of supplies by the cab and shouted into the pipe. "Help! We're down here under the snow. Help! Here we are!"

The giant snow blower moved along the white expanse that was supposed to be a road. Ned Thomas, the driver, carefully guided the big, roaring machine, his eyes searching for familiar landmarks by which to steer.

Beside him sat his work partner, Alex Krueger. Both men studied the space ahead, concentrating on keeping their powerful machine centered on hard, solid ground.

In their wake, they left a cleanly cleared passageway through the drifting snows. A second truck, sporting the markings of the Gallatin County Search and Rescue Squad, followed close behind. It carried two snowmobiles and assorted emergency equipment. Searching for lost travelers was nothing new to the men driving the vehicles. They only hoped they'd find Barry Gordon and Debbie Hanson in time.

The first vehicle sent a steady fountain of snow high into the air. Alex operated the controls of the powerful blower, aiming the spout so as to direct the arching loads of snow away from the road and into areas where they'd be out of the way.

Debbie continued to shout, her mouth pressed against the pipe.

Suddenly, she felt cold snow slam against her face, and the light that had been filtering down the shaft disappeared. The girl fell back into the truck bed, coughing and sputtering, a look of terror in her eyes.

She fumbled for the flashlight and directed its beam at the air shaft. What she saw made her heart stop mid-beat. The pipe had been filled with snow. The very machine sent to save her and Barry had thrown its load high into the air, and, unknown to the drivers, had covered up the only sign of the captives' presence with a fresh blanket of powder. Not only was the light gone, but now the two people buried deep under the drifts were without a fresh supply of air.

Barry closed his eyes, the pain in his chest growing unbearable. He knew Debbie would be unable to get another shaft up through the now hard-packed snows. It was no longer a question of how long before they'd be rescued. It was a question of how long they could stay alive in their icy tomb.

Debbie glanced over at her companion and choked back a sob. The young man didn't hear. He had slipped into unconsciousness.

* * * * *

"They're coming. THEY'RE COMING!" Samantha shouted as she ran down the second floor hallway of the north wing of the Station. She'd been waiting at the window of the room closest to the road that passed above and beside the old hotel.

At first, she'd seen the fountain of snow flowing up and over the trees some distance away. Then suddenly, the lead vehicle had emerged from the man-made blizzard, lights flashing in the early morning gray.

"Joey! John!" Mr. Hanson shouted as he grabbed his pair of snowshoes and stumbled out onto the front porch. "I'll climb up to the road and meet 'em. They'll have another pair of snowshoes for you, John. I talked with the police chief a few minutes ago. He said the rescue squad would be right behind the blower, with snowmobiles and other equipment we might need."

By now the machine was roaring along the road above the Station, its cascade of snow aimed away from the valley and against the side of the mountain. Ned brought the machine to a halt when he saw Mr. Hanson scurrying up the hill toward him.

"I'm sure glad to see you," the lawyer called, extending his hand as the driver hopped down from the work machine.

Ned smiled. "I think we'll be able to continue on up the valley for another two miles or so, toward the Dawson spread." He shouted above the din of the engine. "After that, the snowmobiles will work best on the logging roads." The highway worker pointed at the emergency truck waiting behind the blower.

"We've got two of 'em. Mr. Dawson and a squad member can head into the mountains to dig out Wendy and Merrilee. You and Joey can go back toward the highway with the other. The rescue truck will be tight on your heels."

Mr. Hanson nodded. "Did you see anything at all?"

"Nothing." The man spread his hands in a gesture of helplessness. "The radio dispatcher said no one's found anything along Highway 191—"

"And the police chief just called and said Barry never reached the school," the lawyer interjected. "He and Debbie must've tried for the ranch. That means they've gotta be somewhere between here and the main road." Mr. Hanson started walking in the direction of the emergency vehicle. "We'd better get to work."

"Take this." Ned drew a walkie-talkie from his coat pocket and handed it to Mr. Hanson. "We'll monitor you from the truck. If you find anything, call."

"You'll be the first to know, trust me," the lawyer smiled, then he paused. "They will be OK, won't they?"

Ned nodded. "We'll find them, Tyler. They'll be home in time for lunch."

Mr. Hanson waved weakly and then hurried to lend a hand to the emergency personnel off-loading the snowmobiles. They worked quickly.

Tyler Hanson had a strange feeling in the pit of

his stomach that time might not be on their side. They had to find Barry and Debbie soon. Very soon.

* * * * *

The air in the dark confines of the buried truck grew heavy. Debbie found herself gasping after the slightest exertion. Barry's breathing was steady. He hadn't moved for more than an hour.

"Don't panic!" the girl ordered, trying to convince herself that there was still hope. She lifted the flashlight and shone it around the dark truck bed. "We just need air. That's all. Lots of it up above our heads, so all I've got to do is figure out a way of getting some of it down here. Simple." She closed her eyes. "Not so simple. The passageway is clogged and I can't shove another pipe through the snow. Tried that. Packed too hard."

She rested her head against the cab frame. "The snow has had two days to settle. Then the blower presented us with a fresh load. Who knows how high the new drift is. At least *it* wouldn't be packed hard."

Debbie's chest heaved as her lungs searched for breathable air. She continued to shine the flashlight around the truck bed, not sure of what she was looking for. The beam slipped past the grocery bags, one only half full now. It passed the piles of feed and a collection of leather straps that Barry and Joey were to use to mend some aging harness.

Finally it came to rest on a bundle of smaller PVC pipes, wrapped tightly together with lengths of string. She studied the bundle for a long moment, her mind fighting growing dizziness.

"Pipe. Small pipe." Debbie's head tilted slightly as she continued to gasp for air. "Can't push it through the packed snow. Too hard."

Her eyes closed. "Oh, God, help me. Don't know what to do. Snow's too hard all around. Can't push it through—"

She blinked. "New snow isn't packed. Blower snow's only an hour old." She reached forward, steadying herself with her outstretched hand. "Snow in passageway is new snow. Not packed."

Beads of sweat glistened across the girl's forehead as she crawled along the dark truck bed. "Maybe I can push the smaller pipe up through the big pipe. Maybe I can make a new air passage."

Her hands fumbled with the string that tied the bundles of plastic tubing. "Gotta stay awake. Gotta get some air. Gotta save us."

With her world beginning to spin faster and faster, the girl gathered several of the lengths of pipe. She found the couplings in a nearby box, the same type of couplings Barry had used to join the larger pipes.

Debbie's hands trembled as she twisted the first two lengths together. Her head was pounding now, her brain beginning its one-way journey into oxygen starvation.

"How shall I cap it? Don't have a small piece that

will fit. Snow will get in as I push it through the other pipe." The girl reached up and slipped her woolen ski cap from her head. She held it out in front of her. "There's a cap," she said. Then she began to giggle. "Get it? Cap?"

She started laughing out loud. "That's funny," she chuckled, weaving drunkenly in the darkness. "Need a cap. Got a cap. Right there on my head."

As the oxygen supply continued to dwindle, Debbie wrapped her red cap around the top of the first length of pipe and secured it with a string. She held the plastic tubing out in front of her. "You look like a skinny skier." The girl giggled again, her thoughts fading in and out as she fought the effects of rebreathing her own air. "Up you go, you skinny skier."

The girl pushed the smaller pipe adorned with its woolen cap up into the snow-clogged passageway. The work was not easy. Weaving back and forth, almost losing her balance several times, she managed to attach a third section, then a fourth. By now she was so dizzy that she leaned heavily against the side of the truck bed. She fought waves of nausea.

"Please, Lord," she prayed, her mind dulled with jumbled thoughts and emotions. "Air. Please, air. Gotta get air—"

She fell forward against the pipe and slipped down into a crumpled heap, her face pressed against the open end of the last section of plastic tubing. Her strength was gone, robbed by the carbon dioxide in the buried truck. Before losing consciousness she was able to whisper just two words. "God help."

* * * * *

Wendy looked up from her book and studied the window across the room for a long moment, then returned to her reading.

Seconds later she looked up again. "I heard something," she said.

Merrilee, who was sitting at the dining room table trying to glue a broken saucer back together with some "scientifically improved and space tested" glue, tilted her head slightly. "Just the wind," she yawned.

Wendy shrugged and turned the page. Suddenly they both heard a noise—far away. It sounded like a motor running at high speed. First it would whine, then sputter as if working hard, then run smoothly again.

The two jumped to their feet and hurried up the stairs. They reached the second-floor bedroom window at the same time.

Something was out there all right, and it was coming closer.

Then they saw it—a snowmobile blasting through the drifts on the logging trail beyond the grove of trees that guarded the last bend in the road.

"We're SAVED!" Wendy shouted as she flung open the window. "No more dark nights, with the wind howling like a mad wolf. No more hard floor to sleep on. And—" she closed her eyes savoring the moment, "no more *baked beans!*"

Merrilee grinned broadly as she recognized the passenger on the snowmobile speeding into the yard. "Hurrah for John! My hero!"

Wendy blinked. "And hurrah for whoever's driving. Hey. Didn't any of my family come to save me? Humph. Probably too busy with important things like brushing their teeth or clipping their toenails."

Merrilee laughed as she waved to her husband. "Now, now. Don't be upset. There's only room for two on the snowmobile. Besides, I wouldn't mind if Pueblo the dog came to save us. Just get me back to some place where I can take a shower and sleep on something soft."

Wendy nodded. "You're right. They're probably planning a welcome home party for us as we speak."

The vehicle stopped by the snow-blocked front porch and the driver switched off the engine.

"Hello up there," John called. "You guys all right?"

"A little sunburned, but surviving," Wendy responded cheerfully. "How's everything at the Station?"

A shadow crossed the man's face. "Not too good, I'm afraid. Barry and Debbie never made it back. We don't know where they are. People are out looking for them right now."

"Never made it back?" Merrilee gasped. "You mean—"

"Yeah. Storm got 'em somewhere between Bozeman and the ranch. We believe they got as far as the turnoff, but the road crews haven't found the truck yet. Mr. Hanson and Joey are out searching the stretch between the Station and 191."

Wendy's hands trembled slightly. "Oh, Merrilee. I'm sorry I said what I did about my family not coming to rescue me. Debbie's in real danger and I—"

"It's OK, Wendy," the woman comforted. "You didn't know."

John unstrapped a snowshoe from his back and attached it to his foot. "By the way, this is Doug. He's an emergency medical technician out of Bozeman. Works for the rescue squad. He'll check the two of you out and then drive us, one at a time, back to the Station. Wendy, you'll go first, OK?"

"OK," the girl nodded, then paused. "How's my dad doing, with Debbie missing and all?"

John shook his head. "Let's just say they'd better find her today, and she'd better be safe. It's pretty rough on him." The man smiled gently. "He said to tell you that he loves you very much and for you to pray harder than you've ever prayed before."

Wendy nodded. "Thanks, Mr. Dawson." Turning to Merrilee she said softly, "Will you pray with me? I'm scared."

The two knelt by the window and Wendy closed her eyes tightly. "Our Father in heaven," she whispered, "protect my sister. Keep her safe until someone finds her and Barry. Please, God. I love her. She's my sister and I don't want anything bad to happen to her. Please. Help my dad and Joey find her very, very soon. In Jesus' name, amen."

Merrilee whispered her own "amen" then encircled the youngster in her arms. "God knows where she is. They'll find her. You'll see."

Mr. Dawson studied the two kneeling forms in the upstairs window. After a long moment he called out, "Let's hurry back to the Station so we can welcome Debbie home, OK?"

The girl tried to smile through the fear gripping her young heart. "We'll dig a path from the porch to the snowmobile," she said. "It's pretty deep down there."

Mr. Dawson thrust his loose snowshoe into the drift. It disappeared completely. "Do tell. We've got our work cut out for us. Let's get busy."

Doug and his passenger carefully began to scoop out the snow beside their vehicle as Wendy and Merrilee hurried downstairs. Opening the front door, they started digging away at the drifts that had shut them from the outside world. Wendy worked feverishly as if her actions would somehow assist in the search for her dark-haired missing sister.

* * * * *

Mr. Hanson slowly guided his snowmobile along the snow-blanketed road. The blower had done its work well, blasting a wide path over the old route that connected Shadow Creek Ranch with the main highway three miles to the west.

Joey straddled the machine's back, his feet firmly planted on the runners, fingers gripping his companion's shoulders as he strained to see over the lip of the snow into the drifts that spread out on each side of the road.

Close behind, eyes scanning to the left and right, Don Hixon and Marie Holland strained to catch any sign of the missing vehicle or its young driver and passenger.

"This isn't good," Marie sighed. "They've been out here almost 48 hours. I've seen victims lose their lives in a lot less time."

"I know what you mean," her partner nodded. "Remember last year when we found that couple up in Maudlow? Frozen solid in their car. They'd broken down while out joyriding in a storm. They had moved into the state from Florida and had no idea what cold was. If they'd just taken a few precautions they'd be alive today."

Marie nodded somberly. "These are natives, or at least Barry is. Hope they were better prepared. I wouldn't want to be the one to tell that man up there his daughter won't be coming home for supper— ever."

"You're right. But after two days in a blizzard, I don't hold out much hope. We'd better be prepared for the worst."

The vehicle crept forward as all eyes searched

the roadsides and embankments.

Mr. Hanson twisted the grip on the handle bars and brought the snowmobile to a stop. He reached down and turned the key, allowing the engine to sputter to silence.

He sat heavily on the narrow seat, shoulders sagging. "You see anything, Joey?" he asked.

"Not yet," the lad responded, trying to keep his words hopeful. "We're almost to the main road again, aren't we?"

"Yeah. It's about a quarter mile away. Thought we'd see if we could hear anything."

The lawyer signaled for Don to shut off his truck's motor. The countryside became still as the second engine quieted.

Storm Castle Rock loomed overhead, its proud face of granite bearded with snow. Scattered growths of pine trees thrust green arms out into the morning light, giving the mountain a ragged, disheveled look.

In desperation, Mr. Hanson turned and gazed up at the rocks jutting high into the blue sky overhead. "What did you see?" he pleaded. "Tell me! Did they come this way? Did you notice them? Please tell me."

Joey listened as his friend's voice echoed and re-echoed along the frozen surfaces of the mountainside and across the low, small meadows. "Somebody tell me," the man begged, his voice strained with agony. "Where are they? Where's my little Debbie?"

The boy's eyes filled with tears as his companion's words tore at his heart. He'd never had a father. He'd never known what father love was like. Now, on this narrow, valley road, he was beginning to understand the depth of feeling that a parent has for a child. He'd caught a glimpse of it last spring, when Wendy's horse had come back to the ranch without her. Now the man, his friend, his best friend, was breaking under the weight of another fearful time.

All the words and sermons he'd heard about how God was the Father of everyone on earth were beginning to make sense. Mr. Hanson was demonstrating, on a smaller scale, just how filled with anguish earth's heavenly Father must be as He searches for His children lost in the blizzard of sin.

Joey saw the man fall to his knees, eyes lifted heavenward. "Please," the man pleaded. "We've searched the whole way. They've *got* to be here. They've just got—"

Mr. Hanson paused, studying the tree branches by the side of the road. Joey followed his gaze and noticed several limbs had been snapped in two, as if something heavy had been thrown against them.

The lawyer stumbled to his feet and walked slowly to the edge of the road. Other tree limbs had been broken, all in the same direction. Joey and his companion scrambled up the wall of white snow that bordered the roadway. Don and Marie quickly joined them.

From the top of the bank, the four searchers gazed down into a narrow gully. They recognized that the blower had sprayed snow in this direction as it passed by. But what was most curious was the pattern of destruction through the trees. The broken, twisted limbs and branches pointed like lifeless fingers at an open patch of snow. This was a spot where Joey and Mr. Hanson knew a creek flowed during the summer.

All at once, the man's hand rose trembling and stretched out in front of him. "Look," he whispered.

The others strained to see what their companion was gazing at. There, half hidden in the snow, was a tiny patch of red. Mr. Hanson's voice was hoarse as he spoke. "Debbie . . . Debbie was wearing a red cap when she left. I gave it to her last Christmas."

Don placed his hand on the lawyer's shoulder. "Why don't you let us take care of this, OK?" he said slowly. "You can wait up here on the road."

"NO!" Mr. Hanson said firmly. "She's my daughter. I'll bring her up."

Joey felt sick to his stomach. His hands shook as he helped his friend strap on a pair of snowshoes. Don and Marie ran to the truck and grabbed their own set and hurried back to the side of the road.

Wordlessly, the lawyer eased himself over the lip of the drifts and made his way down into the narrow gully. After what seemed like forever, he reached the spot where the little patch of red jutted from the snow.

"Oh, Debbie," the man whispered. "I'm sorry. I'm so sorry."

He knelt and touched the woolen fibers, totally expecting to feel his beautiful daughter's lifeless head underneath.

Joey saw the man's hand stop, then feel around the cap. The lawyer stood and shouted, "It's attached to some sort of tube. It's Debbie's cap, all right, but how did it get here—"

Mr. Hanson stiffened. "Oh, dear God! It's an air passage. That's what it is." He fell to his knees as Don approached and Marie grabbed the walkie-talkie from her pocket. "It's an air passage from below," the lawyer shouted. "The truck. It's buried. That's what happened. The truck came off the road and broke all those limbs and landed down here. Then the snows covered it up. Hurry! They're buried under here. They may still be alive. HURRY!"

Joey ran to the emergency vehicle and collected an armload of shovels. Moving quickly, he waded through the drifts, his feet sinking deep into the powder as he half fell, half slid down the embankment. Eager hands clutched the tools and began working, following the pipe into the snow.

Mr. Hanson ripped the cap from the tube and shouted down into its dark throat. "DEBBIE! BARRY! WE'RE COMING. WE'RE COMING! HANG ON! JUST HANG ON!"

* * * * *

Wendy saw Grandpa Hanson running for the farm truck as she and the driver of the snowmobile sped down the long driveway toward the Station. Something was up. She knew it.

"Take me to my grandfather, there," she shouted over the din of the conveyance. The driver nodded and altered course to reach the snow-encased farm truck parked by the area the blower had cleared in front of the Station.

Ned was standing nearby, ear pressed against a walkie-talkie. Wendy saw him shake his head, then motion for his companion to follow him.

"What's going on?" the girl called as the snowmobile came to a halt by the porch.

"They think they've found where Barry's truck is," the old man shouted, his hand pulling blocks of snow from his vehicle. " 'Bout a quarter mile from the main road. It's buried."

Wendy gasped. "Buried? Under the snow?"

"Yup." Grandpa Hanson reached out and hugged his youngest granddaughter. "How you doin', Wendy? Glad to see you made it through all right. We kinda figured you would."

"Merrilee and I did fine, once we got some wood for the stove. Have they talked to Debbie?"

"No. There's only an air passage up to the surface, but thank God for that."

Ned and the others added their energies to the task at hand and slowly the old farm truck emerged from the drift. "We've got some more shovels in the

147

blower. We can all help," Ned encouraged. "I've called Bozeman. They're sending a chopper down to Castle Rock. That's where they found the truck. Those two just might need some medical attention when we dig 'em out. Better safe than sorry."

Grandpa Hanson jumped into the farm vehicle and fired up the engine. Wendy and Mr. Krueger scrambled in and together they sped back up the driveway, followed by the ponderous highway blower.

Doug spun his snowmobile round and began his journey back up the mountain toward Merrilee. There were still two people to retrieve from the old homestead.

By the time Wendy and the others arrived at the accident site, Joey, Mr. Hanson, and the emergency crew had just about reached the top of the buried truck. They'd followed the pipe, which could be seen clearly embedded in the wall of snow.

"Daddy!" Wendy called from the road as she shouldered a shovel and started down the embankment.

Mr. Hanson looked up and waved. "Hi, honey. One down, two to go," he called. "I'm so glad to see you." He waded through the drifts and engulfed his daughter in a firm hug. "Are you OK?"

"I'm fine, Daddy," Wendy smiled bravely. "Really. Don't worry about me. Let's just get Debbie and Barry out of there."

The two hurried to the site and began digging,

lifting heavy loads of snow as down, down, down they burrowed.

Every so often, Mr. Hanson would stop and hurry to the pipe, removing a section as it was freed and calling down into the darkness of the plastic tubing. "Debbie? Barry? Can you hear me?"

He'd listen, his ear pressed against the opening, then shake his head to the others and everyone would continue digging. Arms and backs ached, but no one complained. The work they were doing was far too important to worry about hurting muscles.

Below, in the darkness of the snow-covered truck bed, a young girl lay unmoving, her face illuminated by the dimming glow of the flashlight she'd dropped as consciousness had faded. Her face was pressed against the round, hard end of the tube, mouth open, eyes closed. Nearby, Barry lay still on his pile of blankets. There was no sound.

"Debbie? Debbie?" High, filtered words rattled in the pipe. They sounded miles away—miles and miles, like the cry of a hawk in some distant valley. The finger on Debbie's left hand twitched slightly.

"Debbie? Can you hear me?"

The girl's eyes fluttered almost imperceptibly as a few flakes of snow struck her face. The feverish work overhead had loosened some of the powder and it had fallen from the larger pipe resting inches from her nose.

"Barry? Can you hear me? Can you answer?"

That voice. It sounded familiar.

"Daddy?" the girl whispered in the darkness. "Daddy?"

"If you can hear me, say something. Anything." The voice was pleading, almost like someone crying and talking at the same time.

"Daddy?" Debbie strained to speak, but her throat was dry, unresponsive. Slowly her hand moved from her side and paused just above her cheek. With all the strength she could muster, she bumped her fingers against the pipe.

Mr. Hanson froze, his eyes opening wide. "Wait!" he ordered. The digging stopped.

"Debbie? Barry? Can you hear me? Did you move the air passage? I felt it move."

The girl's hand rose again and struck the plastic casing by her face. Mr. Hanson felt the jolt. "SOME-ONE'S ALIVE DOWN THERE!" he shouted, tears mingling with the cold sweat on his face. "I felt the pipe move. I felt it move twice!" He paused. "There. It bumped again. Someone is hitting the pipe."

"WE'RE COMING!" he shouted into the mouth of the air passage. "HANG ON. WE'RE COMING!"

The workers began digging with renewed determination. There was hope in each heart. Somebody was alive in the buried truck. If one was still breathing, maybe both were.

Debbie's eyes blinked open. She could now hear strange sounds overhead—scraping, bumping, voices, beautiful voices calling her name.

Her lungs burned as she drew in a deep breath.

Cold, fresh air was flowing from the pipe by her face—oxygen, life-giving oxygen.

She tried to move but felt terribly dizzy. Slowly, painfully, she drew in breath after breath, feeling warmth return to her fingers and toes, her arms, legs, and chest.

Pressing her mouth against the pipe she called out in a voice growing in strength. "Daddy. We're here. We're here in the truck."

The man heard the call and cradled the mouth of the pipe in his trembling hands. "Debbie? Did you say something?" He held his breath as the others gathered around.

"Help us," he heard a weak voice call from somewhere far below. "Help us, Daddy."

The lawyer sank to his knees, crying, tears streaming down his face. "Thank You, God. Oh, thank You." He moved to the pipe. "Is Barry OK? Is he alive?"

Debbie nodded sluggishly. "He's hurt. But I think he's still alive. Yes. I can hear him breathing. Hurry, Daddy. Hurry and save us."

"THEY'RE BOTH ALIVE!" the man cried out, grabbing each worker, one after another. "They're both alive, but we must hurry. Barry's hurt and Debbie sounds very weak." He grabbed his shovel and began digging, almost out of control. "Hurry, everybody, hurry. My little girl is alive. SHE'S ALIVE!"

High overhead, a helicopter thundered into view.

It passed over the top of Castle Rock like a dark bird. The pulsating sound of its rotors rushed down the cliffs and settled on the little valley below. The pilot could see activity in a gully by the cleared road. He searched for a place to set down and decided Highway 191, just off to the right, would be best.

With skillful hands he guided his powerful machine and came to rest in a blowing cloud of snow at the turnoff. He'd await further orders there.

CHAPTER 8

WHISPERS

❂ ❂ ❂

Clank. Joey's shovel hit something hard, almost jerking the tool out of his gloved hands.

"Hey," he shouted to the others working all around him. "I think I've got somethin' here."

The workers hurried over to the spot where the boy was kneeling. He pushed aside several handfuls of snow, revealing a shiny expanse of metal. Others dropped to their knees and started digging with their hands, widening the hole and revealing the battered roof of a truck cab.

Mr. Hanson thrust his hand into the snow beside the pipe and felt his fingers break through into open space. Eagerly he pushed aside the last barrier that separated him from his daughter. He dropped onto his stomach to peer into the dark cavity where the driver-side window used to be.

Sunlight filtered into the cab and sent shadowy shafts of light into the dark recesses of the covered bed beyond. He saw a pale, dirt-smudged face and tearful eyes staring back at him.

"Debbie?" he said softly. "I love you."

The girl started to cry as her father pushed his body through the opening and slid into the cab. "Do you know that? I love you." He repeated his gentle greeting as he crawled to where his daughter lay crumpled just inside the dimly lit bed.

Debbie wrapped her arms around the man and held him close for a long, long moment. They wept silently together in the confines of the truck, lost in the unspeakable joy of being reunited after two days of bottomless fear.

Debbie kissed her father's face and smiled into his eyes. "It's not your fault, Daddy," she said, realizing the burden her father carried when anything bad happened to his precious daughters.

The man smiled. "Have I ever told you how much you mean to me?"

Debbie nodded. "That's what kept me going," she whispered. "I knew you'd come and save us. I just knew it."

Mr. Hanson touched his daughter's cheek with the back of his fingers. "If anything had happened to you—anything—"

"I'm OK, Daddy," she said quietly. "But we gotta

help Barry. He's hurt pretty badly."

The lawyer moved to the wrangler's side. "How did it happen?"

"He slammed into the steering wheel," the girl said. "I think something's broken inside—ribs and stuff."

"Can you get around OK?" the man asked.

"I think so."

The two slowly made their way into the cab, then out into the bright, cold sunlight. A cheer arose from those gathered about the small opening as Debbie emerged, shielding her eyes from the brightness.

Gentle hands guided her up to the road, where she was placed on a stretcher. An emergency medical technician began asking her questions and carefully examining her, looking for any signs of hidden injuries.

"I'm OK. Really," she said. "Just help my friend in the truck. He's hurt."

Once it was determined that Debbie was in no immediate danger, all hands joined in the effort to free the unconscious wrangler still buried in the wreck.

Mr. and Mrs. Gordon, summoned from Bozeman, arrived just in time to see their son lifted carefully out of the entombed vehicle and strapped to an air-transport stretcher.

The helicopter rose over the trees and hovered above the accident site. A crewman lowered a long cable, which was quickly grabbed by a member of the rescue squad below. Skillfully they secured the injured man's stretcher to the cable. Everyone held their breath as Barry's warmly wrapped form floated heavenward and was guided in through the open door of the noisy aircraft. With a wave, the pilot of the helicopter adjusted his control yokes and the machine bowed forward and sped away. A medical trauma team at the city hospital had been alerted and were standing by, waiting for their patient to arrive.

As Debbie sat watching the aircraft disappear from view, she felt someone tap her on the shoulder. Turning, she gazed into the eyes of her father. "Better put this on," he said, handing her a red ski cap. "Don't want you to catch cold."

The girl chuckled wearily and held the woolen hat out in front of her. "One of the best Christmas presents I ever received," she said. "Now I just need some gloves to match."

"Oh, brother," Wendy groaned, slipping up beside her father. "Same ol' Debbie. Two days in a deep-freezer and she's still worried about color coordination."

"Hey, Wendy," the older girl smiled, "did you make it through the storm OK?"

"Piece of cake—or should I say, piece of baked beans."

"Huh?"

The younger girl laughed. "I'll tell you about it later, after the doctor finishes transplanting all your organs or whatever he's going to do to you." She paused. "I'm glad you're all right. I was worried."

Debbie blinked. "You? Worried about me? Boy, that storm must've rattled your brains or something."

Wendy frowned. "You're my sister and I . . . I . . . I love you."

Mr. Hanson grinned and ruffled his youngest daughter's hair. "Keep that thought for the next 50 years."

The girl giggled. "Ask Joey how *he* survived the storm. Grandpa said he had to eat horse food."

"It weren't too bad," the boy called from nearby, where he was helping the rescue squad load the snowmobile onto their truck. "'Cept, now, every time I see a straight stretch of road I have this irresistible urge to gallop."

Debbie laughed. "Sounds like you guys had a tough time, too."

"Nah," Wendy said, waving her hand. "It was nothin'."

As the rescue squad gently helped the dark-haired girl into their vehicle for the drive to the hospital, Wendy leaned forward and asked, "Hey, Debbie. When you were buried down there, where'd you go to the bathroom?"

Mr. Hanson pulled his youngest daughter away from the truck. "Wendy! Leave your poor sister alone. She's trying to recover."

Debbie laughed a tired laugh. "I'll never tell," she teased.

The lawyer reached up and touched his daughter's hand. "We'll be at the hospital just as soon as we can get there. We're going to pick up Grandma and Lizzy. Oh, and Samantha told me on the radio to tell you that if you want, she can bring Pueblo. She says he's very worried about you."

The truck pulled away as Debbie grinned and waved. "I love you guys," she called. "Hurry and come take me home."

The group returned her wave and stood in the empty roadway for a long time, listening to the grind of gears and race of the distant motor.

Slowly the tired rescuers walked back to the old farm truck—all, that is, except Mr. Hanson.

Quietly he slipped from the others and stood looking down into the gully. Packed snow circled a small opening in the drifts where portions of Barry's truck jutted from the white, icy blanket. The man closed his eyes. "Thank You, God," he whispered. "Thank You for keeping Your hand over my precious little girl and Wrangler Barry." He paused. "Lord, make me stronger than I am. Build my faith so that when troubles come, I'll lean more on You and less on fear. Forgive my untrusting heart. Please, Lord. Amen."

The man felt a touch on his shoulder as Grandpa Hanson joined him by the edge of the road. "Faith's a funny thing, Tyler," the old man said softly. "Right when you need it most, it seems to be the weakest. That's when you have to listen, listen for God's whispers."

"Even in a blizzard?"

"Especially then," the older man nodded. "Joey, Wendy, Debbie, you, me—I'm sure we all heard God speak to us in our own ways during the past 48 hours." Grandpa Hanson turned. "I think we should talk about it in the days and weeks to come. Whatta ya say, Tyler?"

The lawyer nodded. "I thought my heart would break, Dad. I didn't think I'd make it through . . . not knowing."

"That's what sin does," Grandpa Hanson continued. "It breaks good people's hearts. But God's an expert at picking up the pieces and bringing confidence back into our lives. We can't live in fear of tomorrow. We have to have faith that no matter what tomorrow brings, God will be by our side, ready and willing to help us get through our times of greatest fear."

"You're right," Mr. Hanson sighed. "I need to learn to listen for the whispers. I guess my fear got in the way—sorta blocked everything else out."

The old man smiled. "Come on, one and only son of mine. Let's get back to the Station and round everybody up. We gotta head into town. Our little Debbie's been separated from us long enough."

The two men hurried to the farm truck and brought the engine to life. As the vehicle roared up the valley toward the distant ranch, silence once again settled over the gully. Storm Castle Rock loomed overhead, its stone face indifferent to what had happened at its feet.

But the inhabitants of Shadow Creek Ranch had learned, once again, that there's a Presence beyond the towering mountains, past the dark line of clouds, above the rumble of thunder.

Up there, where peace reigns, is a God who speaks to all His children, sometimes in words loud and clear. And sometimes in whispers carried by the wind.